THE WASTE DEITY

Rijuta Gupta

Published By

Redgrab Books Pvt. Ltd.
942, Mutthiganj, Prayagraj, 211003
www.redgrabbooks.com
contact@redgrabbooks.com

Price in india : 250/- INR

First published by Redgrab Books in 2024
Copyright © 2024 Rijuta Gupta
Printed and bound in India
Cover Design & Typesetting by Redgrab Books team

ISBN : 978-93-95697-67-5

Dedication

To my parents for shielding my quirkiness
and to my daughter for cherishing it.

For all the waste generators
and the waste managers of this world

CONTENTS

PROLOGUE

Without beating around the bush, let me commence the story of a bereaved mother who sets off on a journey to find a cure for a deadly fungus and ends up becoming the Waste Goddess.

Chapter 1
A Tragic Beginning

The death of a child is a traumatic experience. When the reason of death is a fungal infection, it causes untold grief to the parents because it is a loss that could have been prevented.

The Bountiful family is one of the most affluent families of the country, but their wealth failed to save the infant. It was the third day of the tragedy. The household staff was wearing their regular uniform. A different colour was assigned for each day of the week. There was also a difference in the colours of scarves and caps according to the work undertaken by the staff—white scarves and caps for cooks and food tasters, mauve for personal care assistants, blue for janitors, and so on. Today, all of them were wearing a separate mourners' apron over their uniforms.

Most of the visitors reached the prayer hall without attracting anyone's attention. But there were a few among them who managed to turn people's heads with their mourning ensemble. There was also someone who was looking way more beautiful than usual. From the moment this lady alighted from her car and entered the prayer hall, every pair of eyes followed her—some in admiration and some in contempt, some stealing glances out of the corners of their eyes and some stared at her unreservedly.

There was a constant stream of mourners. They expressed grief though not necessarily in proportion to how affected they were. However, it would be unfair to dismiss their sympathies entirely. The tragedy evoked pity even in the heart of an arch-rival.

It had been more than a decade since I inherited the job of Chief

Security Officer of the Bountiful family. Along with it, I was also the heir to a network of people, the eyes and ears that my father had cultivated during his years of service. I continued to add to this network which provided me with a reliable source of information. It was through this network and my own observations that I concluded that this family did not have any arch-enemy.

"Had she been my child, I would not have left any stone unturned to save her," said a teary-eyed rival. "This world is full of top-rated doctors and I know a few of them personally. One must not hesitate to ask for help during a time of crisis."

Mr. Foeman's tears were sincere and so was his rivalry. He had placed himself in the middle of the room to attract an audience. Everyone understood that he was undermining the family's effort at saving their child. But no one could blame him for uttering such a statement in a raised voice. He was a habitual user of a high-pitched voice and always liked to share his piece of mind with as many people as he possibly could.

Junior Mrs. Bountiful, the mother of the dead baby, removed her child's memorial picture from the stand and clutched it to her chest. Until Mr. Foeman's provocation, she refused to believe that her baby was dead. Tears stained her clothes but she would not stop crying.

"I couldn't save my child. What kind of a mother am I?" Junior Mrs. Bountiful repeated over and over.

Her husband tried to embrace her, but she shrugged him off.

"You couldn't save your child. What kind of a father are you?" she asked him. Mr. Bountiful did not pay any heed to the accusation directed towards him. He was relieved that, at last, his wife has accepted the loss of their child. He looked at Mr. Foeman and nodded his head in gratitude. Even though Mr. Foeman did it inadvertently, he had brought Junior Mrs. Bountiful out of her emotional numbness.

Mr. Foeman is a fine-looking gentleman, but he is no match to Mr. Bountiful's charm. In spite of his sorrow, Mr. Bountiful was suitably dressed in a crumpled shirt. Crumpling is the demand of the occasion and the chosen fabric had the perfect number of creases. He and his wife made a great pair. They were blessed with good looks and had an impeccable dress sense.

"Hush Puff is one of the best hospitals in the world. The hospital has specialists from all over the globe. What more can one ask for?" said another grief-stricken mourner. He had waited for young Mrs. Bountiful's wailing to subside. He did not address anyone in particular but his voice was loud enough to reach everyone present in the room. However, Junior Mrs. Bountiful was engrossed in caressing the baby's portrait.

A few photographs of the baby were clicked in the Neonatal Intensive Care Unit. A photograph of a sick child does not make a good memorial picture. Hence, the painter of the memorial portrait received specific instruction to imagine their baby in full health and life so that the family can cherish a lifelong memory.

I had seen this gentleman, the one who just spoke. He would sometimes visit the resident office of Senior Mrs. Bountiful. She was the grandmother of the deceased baby. Her stoic silence could never deter the gentleman from showing his uncalled-for affection. It was not my job to observe these things, but I was concerned about the well-being of my employer. She and her family were rich and generous as long as one understood that affluence and generosity had their limits. I understood it very well and, therefore, received a lot more insight than what other people did.

The name of the gentleman was Peeptown and he was an

affection seeker. Affection seekers are extremely dangerous if their affections are not reciprocated. So, like an able businessperson, Senior Mrs. Bountiful kept him around at a safe distance. This was the first time he was allowed to enter the family home. Grief provided him an excellent excuse to develop proximity.

"This morning, I went to Hush Puff hospital to seek clarity. Instead, I witnessed secrecy," said Peeptown.

Reflexively, I turned towards Senior Mrs. Bountiful. She signalled to me and I moved towards Peeptown to prevent him from speaking further. Before I could navigate through the mourners, however, he took a cursory glance around the room and continued speaking.

"If all specialists say that it is a fungal infection then I am no one to contest it," he said. "But it couldn't have been an ordinary fungus and the Bountiful family is entitled to know the exact reason for their irreplaceable loss."

I stood beside Peeptown. But he was unmindful of my presence.

"The hospital ripped out ceiling, plaster and floor tiles in its newly renovated building. There was intense cleaning going on with sophisticated equipment. The area was cordoned off for visitors and the hospital staff evaded any query," he continued. "Since the ripping of interiors was carried out in and around the Neonatal Intensive Care Unit where the baby had been kept, I am sure it is related to our ill fortune. Do any of you still think that an ordinary fungus can wreak such havoc?"

Fear overshadowed sympathy. If all the riches in the world could not ensure a cure for this fungal infection, it must be a deadly fungus. Amidst the realisation of getting infected by this lethal fungus, visitors were eager to leave the Bountiful House. The prayer meeting was already over and there was no reason to stay behind. The charming lady was the first one to make the move and others followed her out. Peeptown was the only one who remained with the family.

Junior Mrs. Bountiful was taken to her room along with the portrait that she refused to part with. Her three-year-old daughter had also tagged alongside her. Senior Mrs. Bountiful remained seated; a picture of poise.

"What else have you seen?" asked Senior Mrs. Bountiful.

"I haven't seen more than what I have already told," replied Peeptown. "However, I withheld one thing. It isn't just today that I went to the hospital. I began my investigation immediately after they announced the untimely demise of our little angel."

He removed his glasses and cleaned them. I was not sure whether he was wiping off tears or dirt.

"What do you suggest now?" asked the elder lady.

"The hospital must have tested all of you for the fungal infection."

"We all tested negative," intervened Mr. Bountiful.

"I am sure of that," Peeptown responded and once again turned towards the lady. "We can begin with an analysis of your test reports and try to find some clues. We will also approach the hospital administration to obtain whatever information is available to them. However, I believe, most of the hospital staff is a bunch of clueless people and might disappoint us. If that happens, I will share with you the subsequent plan of action."

Senior Mrs. Bountiful looked at Peeptown enquiringly. He responded, "I don't wish to create panic, but you must be prepared for a long journey ahead."

I doubted this fellow was going overboard with his dramatics to gain my employer's attention.

Chapter 2
The Axe Effect

Senior Mrs. Bountiful had always understood the importance of splendour without being ostentatious. She was leaving the house on the fourth day of mourning and had to extract as much information from the Hush Puff's administration as she possibly could. Keeping in mind the gravity of the situation, the dress designer and assistants created a suit that did not seek attention but was showcasing authority. The lady left for the hospital in an elegant ivory coloured suit worn with a Burano lace scarf.

Senior Mrs. Bountiful had sought a meeting with the Supervisory Board and the Expert Committee of Hush Puff hospital simultaneously. They had agreed to meet at a short notice, the pretext being the sensitivity and urgency of the matter.

Apart from providing brief inputs, as and when required by the lady, Peeptown had proven to be a non-interfering associate during the meeting. His information was well researched, making it difficult for the hospital administration to indulge in whataboutery. The Committee sought a week to compile a comprehensive report about the infection, containing all the known cases, facts and other reference material available around the world.

Senior Mrs. Bountiful praised Mr. Peeptown after coming home. She graciously admitted to her family that she had always underestimated his abilities. Accepting one's mistake is a lesson I had learnt from my employer. I am not ashamed to admit that I was wrong in doubting Peeptown, I beg your pardon, Mr. Peeptown.

Many things were happening during the week after Senior Mrs.

Bountiful's visit to the hospital. But the most important matter was to solve the mystery behind the baby's death. Mr. Peeptown failed to remain in touch for the whole week and Senior Mrs. Bountiful began to doubt his dependability.

Mr. Peeptown made up for it, however, by being present at home well within time, winning my employer's confidence back. After receiving the report from the hospital and quickly scrutinizing it, Senior Mrs. Bountiful handed over the voluminous and dreary document to Mr. Peeptown to make sense of it. He willingly took it from her and returned exactly a week after to present the gist of the hospital handout.

"Callousa Attapata is a type of fungus that was first identified a decade back. In recent years, it has emerged in over forty countries across the globe, mostly in hospitals, affecting patients with weak immunity. After entering the bloodstream, it can cause severe infection that may lead to multiple organ failure. This fungus is resistant to major antifungal drugs making its treatment difficult. Special laboratory tests are required to identify it because standard laboratory methods might misidentify it and lead to wrong or delayed treatment. Apart from being thermo-tolerant and salt-tolerant, the fungus is too obstinate to be eradicated once it appears in a facility," Mr. Peeptown said, looking up from the document. "This explains why they ripped off the hospital ceilings and floors."

Everyone nodded.

"It is a relatively new fungal infection for researchers worldwide. In want of further studies and to avoid scaring the public, its outbreak is either played down or hushed up. It means, I was unnecessarily harsh on the Hush Puff team," Mr. Peeptown continued.

"It also means that we may never know how our child could have been saved," my employer said.

After a brief pause she spoke again, "I wonder how it matters when we have already lost…"

"Don't say anything further," Junior Mrs. Bountiful interrupted. After accepting the death of her baby, it was still difficult for her to hear about what happened. Her husband's caress would have comforted her, but he was not at home. Her mother-in-law suggested that she may leave the conversation if she wanted. Junior Mrs. Bountiful decided to stay put.

"Shall we abandon our investigation?" Mr. Peeptown asked.

"What are our options?" asked the younger Mrs. Bountiful.

Mr. Peeptown looked at Senior Mrs. Bountiful and got the approval to proceed.

"We can build a team of researchers or doctors. But to find suitable candidates, we need professional help," Mr. Peeptown replied.

He simultaneously opened a file on his laptop containing shortlisted international detective agencies. Each of the agencies had a more or less similar infrastructure, resources and foreign collaborations. All of them were renowned names in their field. However, one name appeared in different coloured font.

Meanwhile, Mr. Bountiful also joined in and, along with the ladies, was looking towards Mr. Peeptown to listen about the highlighted detective agency.

"A few years back, the owner of this firm had a botched-up nose and lips surgery. She confined herself at home and that resulted in further build-up of frustration. Her parents turned out to be her pillar of strength and, by the time she fully recovered, her career perspective changed. She was no longer interested in getting into the glamour industry and decided to join her father's detective agency," Mr. Peeptown said, opening another file with a pre-surgery and a post-surgery picture of the lady.

Attires of the lady were different, but she looked exactly the same in both photographs.

"Are you playing a joke?" asked Mr. Bountiful. Unlike his mother, Mr. Bountiful had always been fond of Mr. Peeptown. This was the first time I saw him annoyed at the visitor.

"How is this information and the photographs relevant to our case?" intervened Junior Mrs. Bountiful.

As a mother, she must have been inclined to focus only on finding out more about her baby's illness and how they lost the battle in saving it. Even otherwise, a wife should not let her husband get intrigued by another woman, especially if she's extraordinarily beautiful.

"I am sharing this information to explain why this lady will put in her best efforts in helping us."

"Okay, continue," said the young Mrs. Bountiful, reluctantly giving the go-ahead.

"She filed a case of medical negligence against her doctor but lost. The doctor proved that he merely pretended to have conducted the surgery so that the lady wouldn't approach any other cosmetic surgeon. He knew that no one could make the lady more beautiful than she already was and wanted to save her from deforming her face.

"The judge released the doctor with an order to pay the lady an amount equal to the fees with interest. The doctor willingly paid the amount and also expressed his love for the lady."

"Did they marry?" asked Senior Mrs. Bountiful. Mr. Peeptown nodded.

"But her name reads Miss Axe Effect," pointed Junior Mrs. Bountiful. "It's a strange name with a misleading title. Can we trust such a person?"

"She changed her name after the court case because she believed that the doctor had indeed chiselled her face, although to good effect. She credits axe effect for her enhanced beauty," Mr. Peeptown said, laughing. "Her husband treats her as his lover rather than his wife. So, Miss Axe Effect has not yet come to terms with her marital status and continues using her previous title."

"You know a lot about her," remarked Senior Mrs. Bountiful.

"It is my job to meet and understand people. All my life I have been doing that," Mr. Peeptown said.

"How is she useful for our case?"

"Although Miss Axe Effect has married Dr. Axe, she continues to harbour a grudge against his profession. Even with their best intentions, doctors have ample opportunities to fool people. Therefore, whenever there is a case involving the medical fraternity, she puts her heart and soul into solving it."

Senior Mrs. Bountiful approved Miss Axe's appointment as their detective but her son questioned, "Mom, isn't she too pretty to be a good detective?"

"Beauty is an asset and in our case, it has an added advantage," said his mother. "My son will remain interested in the case till we reach its logical conclusion and my daughter-in-law will get busy keeping an eye on her husband instead of nourishing her sorrow."

Junior Mrs. Bountiful frowned and took a deep breath.

"Are you angry at me?" her mother-in-law asked her.

"Yes. Why do you think I shouldn't be sorrowful?"

"Because you are rich, young and beautiful."

"That doesn't take away my right to mourn my loss."

"Your loss doesn't snatch away your right to live either. So, stop arguing and resume living."

Junior opened her mouth and shut it. A hesitant smile floated across her face.

* * *

Having discussed Miss Axe Effect's suitability as a detective, they decided to make their way to her office.

The entrance opens into multiple single-room accommodations with common facilities like a pantry-cum-kitchen, washrooms, a lounge and a library. The premises don't have the visible features of an office compound, but Mr. Peeptown assured the Bountiful family that it was indeed Miss Axe Effect's office.

"Why did she design her office as a housing complex," Senior Mrs. Bountiful asked. Before Mr. Peeptown could reply, she got an answer from a message on a wall: "Going back home is an option, not a compulsion. Work as long as you want to."

While the lady was contemplating, someone hands over a slip that reads: "The purpose is not to provide employees an escape from their family, but to give them comfort when they have to work longer."

Senior Mrs. Bountiful turned towards a mirror hanging on the wall and scrutinized her face. "How could someone know that I was thinking about the impact of office-cum-house arrangement on employees' family life," she spoke in a whisper. Her son shrugged his shoulder.

Senior Mrs. Bountiful took a few deep breaths and quickened her pace towards Miss Axe Effect's cabin.

Miss Effect was not only strikingly gorgeous but had a refreshingly unique fashion style. An aesthetically pleasing combination of dull grey and fluorescent orange on her dress showed that Miss Effect was good at experimenting with colours. On minute inspection, stitches, slits and curves appeared in the right places.

Senior Mrs. Bountiful was about to speak something before she received a text message from Miss Effect on her cellphone, "Wearing a black hat, overcoat, and dark glasses doesn't make someone a good detective."

Senior Mrs. Bountiful could only stare at the detective open-mouthed. Writings on the wall, the paper slip, and the text message must have tricked her mind into believing that Miss Axe Effect possessed supernatural powers to read a person's mind.

Meanwhile, handsome Mr. Bountiful was occupied in analysing beautiful Miss Axe's nose and lips. His lovely wife was observing whether his sight shifted beyond that.

"I am glad all of you found time to visit my office," said Miss Effect. "I understand it's difficult to hold oneself back after hearing about me."

Mr. Bountiful shifted his gaze. One of the Bountiful ladies rubbed her forehead to cover her eyes and the other searched her purse for nothing. The Bountiful family had always been the cynosures of all eyes and here was someone who had rightly guessed their keenness to meet her.

"Mr. Peeptown had handed over a copy of the hospital report and explained your position to me. I will get in touch with you as and when I have an update," said the beautiful detective, relieving the family of their embarrassment.

* * *

"All of you must resume your regular work. Rest assured that I will keep you posted regarding this matter," said Mr. Peeptown.

During his absence, Senior Mrs. Bountiful decided to follow his advice.

The grief of a young mother, the charm and supernatural powers of a beautiful lady and the affection for a newly found well-wisher kept the matter burning during the days that followed. With each passing day, the Bountiful family members talked less and less about the baby, but at each moment they expected a call to know how the investigation was progressing.

It was almost a month since the baby died. The family had regained some composure and was coming to terms with their loss. With calmer minds, a realisation dawned upon them—they were venturing into something of great consequence and it would be beneficial for the whole of humankind. At first, they were agitated and excited at the prospect. Gradually, they accepted it as an opportunity to rise above their limitations and pledged not to give up before finding a cure for the deadly virus.

Mr. Peeptown came home to accompany Senior Mrs. Bountiful to the meeting with Miss Axe Effect. A few of the staff members giggled at his arrival, but my employer's focus was on receiving her guest with utmost warmth. These staff members had a terrible knack for spreading malicious gossip. I chose not to censor them because it was impossible to rein them in and any attempt to do so would make my work environment unconducive.

Once again, Mr. Bountiful and his wife accompanied his mother to the detective's office. A family that investigates together, stays together.

Chapter 3

The Pilgrim and The Adventurer

The Bountiful family along with Mr. Peeptown gathered at Axe's office to finalise a team of experts to expedite studies on Callousa Attapata, the deadly fungus. Microbiologist, fungus, infections, researches, data analysis, disease propagation and prevention—all these terms were recurring in Miss Axe Effect's presentation. Her unwavering professionalism had taken the shine off her beauty and everyone was sitting attentively so as not to miss a word coming out of her mouth.

Miss Effect pressed the presentation clicker and the title read: INGENIOUS EXPERTS. Photographs of two men appeared on the screen—Dr. Nestor, Medical Microbiologist and Dr. Spunk, Research Scientist, Pathogenic Fungi.

Miss Axe pressed the clicker again. The title of the next slide was PATHOGENIC FUNGI IN WASTE-PICKERS.

"These two experts are known for their affinity for the poor. Instead of exploring tourist spots, they visit slums in different countries during their vacations. They have observed that every city in developing countries has at least one mountain of garbage and these man-made mountains are the workplace for thousands of people," informed Miss Effect. "Dr. Nestor and Dr. Spunk sensed an opportunity of finding varieties of fungi at these dumpyards because medical waste is also dumped along with the municipal waste. As expected, they found Callousa Attapata on the skin of waste-pickers.

"The shedding of the fungus along with the skin of an infected waste-picker contaminates the surroundings. Further, the lack of testing or isolation of diseased waste-pickers ensures unhindered multiplication of the infection. The large number of infected people is a great advantage for any medical researcher who wants to reach a reliable conclusion. The expert duo sweated and slaved to carry out the fungal study on a variety of human beings across age, gender, ethnicity and geographic distribution. Since these human beings belonged to a vulnerable section of the society, it struck the right chord with the academic community and their study has been declared a superhit."

Another Slide: PROPOSAL—Carrying out an extensive study on Waste-pickers in Dupli City.

"Keeping in mind your motive for undertaking this study, their main focus will be on prevention and treatment of the infection caused by Callousa Attapata," said Miss Axe Effect to the Bountiful family.

The presentation moved forward and the last slide title read: THEIR INDUCEMENT—Opportunity to work amid poor with no fund constraint.

"After their preliminary studies, they will propose more team members, preferably local experts. Before that, we must arrange the necessary administrative approvals," informed Miss Axe Effect.

It was turning out to be bigger than what the Bountiful family had anticipated. Destiny had chosen them to serve mankind.

"I'll make sure they optimize time and other resources at their disposal," assured Miss Effect. "Once the treatment for Callousa Attapata is found, your pharma unit too will reap the benefit."

Miss Axe Effect had explained her reasons behind choosing these two experts and no one questioned her. In fact, the possibility of a financial gain brought a broad smile on Senior Mrs. Bountiful's face.

* * *

Bountiful business portfolio primarily included fast moving consumer goods and pharmaceuticals, apart from a nationwide retail store chain. Junior Mrs. Bountiful was on intermittent bereavement leave and was irregular in attending to her official work. Her mother-in-law reminded her that businesses are not run on sentimentalities and that they must set an example to their employees through their discipline and steadfastness.

My employer followed what she preached. A few years back, she lost her husband and, two days after losing him, she went on a pilgrimage to shed her sorrow and resumed her duties.

Senior Mrs. Bountiful also understood that one must continue to learn new things. She encouraged her daughter-in-law to accompany Dr. Spunk and Dr. Nestor on their first expedition to the waste-pickers' colony adjacent to a dumpyard. This expedition would mark the commencement of their fungal probe.

Junior Mrs. Bountiful readily agreed. A team of videographers was deployed to shoot the entire study tour, which could be used later for reference purposes. The team had been instructed to work without exposing their presence to the young Bountiful lady and the fungal experts.

The baby, who spent its life only in the hospital ICU, was fast becoming a memory. A Neonatal Intensive Care unit with various kinds of pediatric equipment and specialists could not save the infant. The comfort of soundproof flooring and indirect lighting could not sooth the tiny body with tubes and wires attached all over it. No one in the family brought out actual photographs of the baby that were clicked at the hospital because those photographs reminded them of their helpless days and vain efforts.

The memorial picture was placed in the living room. Junior

Mrs. Bountiful had kept a few smaller copies at various places in her bedroom where no one else could see—under the pillow, in drawers or behind the mirror. In the memorial picture, the baby looked so hearty and happy that it became difficult to recall its illness. While others were busy with their regular work, the mother began her grief-stricken investigation. For her, grief had become more of a habit.

* * *

The car halted at the designated meeting spot. The Shoddy Slum visitors would gather here before proceeding with their work. Junior Mrs. Bountiful asked her assistant and chauffeur to remain inside the car and stepped out alone. She was wearing a full-coverage outfit with a pair of sneakers. As usual, there was no compromise on style, which was kept minimal and suitable for the occasion.

Dr. Spunk and Dr. Nestor, both fungal experts, were already there. There was another person with the expert duo—Mr. Candid, their tour guide. Mr. Candid was a waste contractor who hired people for collecting waste from residents and he sold the collected waste to waste handlers. On Miss Axe Effect insistence, he had taken up the work of guiding people through the by-lanes of poverty. He was extremely nervous because he had no prior experience as a tour guide.

Junior Mrs. Bountiful's phone rang.

"I haven't arranged a translator and want you to take up this task," said Miss Axe from the other side of the line. "Please don't get offended. It will help you build rapport with the people living in the slum and understand things better from the researchers' point of view."

Junior Mrs. Bountiful remained silent.

"There's no compulsion, Mrs. Bountiful. Just a slight gesture from you and I will get off from my car.'"

The rich lady looked around, saw a car and smiled. Then, she turned her attention to Mr. Candid after greeting Dr. Nestor and Dr. Spunk.

"Ma'am, I have discussed poverty tourism with one of my acquaintances. He has explained how to conduct an engaging tour in a slum. In his slum, most of the residents are accustomed to being looked at. Here in Shoddy Slum, however, no one has been exposed to the curious eyes of poverty onlookers. So, I request all of you to be discreet while clicking pictures," warned Mr. Candid.

A text message flashed on Junior Mrs. Bountiful's phone screen: "Don't respond. Convey what he has just said to the two researchers. – Miss Axe Effect."

The rich lady translated precisely what she had heard.

"We are not tourists," Dr. Spunk blurted out in defense. Then he looked at Dr. Nestor for an explanation. The latter began to scroll through his digital tablet. Nestor did not seem to be in hurry to speak and Dr. Spunk did not prevail upon his partner to speak. Meanwhile, Junior Mrs. Bountiful performed her task as a translator.

A couple of minutes later, Dr. Nestor placed his digital tablet in front of everyone present. There was an old scanned photograph featuring a kid in an oversized school uniform and neatly combed hair. The surrounding shown in the photograph was as impoverished as Shoddy Slum, with closely-packed decrepit houses and open, haphazard sewerage adorning narrow and dusty passages. But the people in the background were of different ethnicity. It was evident that while people might look different, poverty looked the same in all parts of the world.

"I've spent my entire childhood here," Dr. Nestor finally spoke. "As a child, I was taught that contentment is the key to happiness. But

I used to wonder if contentment is genuinely a virtue, then why does everyone put dreamers and achievers on a pedestal?

"My experiences showed me that contentment is a useful concept for poor parents because it saves them from the regular frustration of declining their children's demands. They label it as a virtue to disguise their incapacity or vulnerability.

"I, however, was neither discontent nor did I set aside my dreams. I have achieved some success and am living a reasonably luxurious life. However, when I visit a new city or a country, I am drawn towards its shanties. These shanties reflect my soul and, like a pilgrim, my head bows in reverence. These places have become shrines for me."

After his partner explained his relation with poverty, Dr. Spunk said, "You know Mrs. Bountiful, initially, Dr. Nestor dissuaded me from following him to slums. But ultimately he gave in to my entreaties and took me in as his companion."

"Because you were seeking adventure in poverty. Facing uncertainty regarding meals or surviving extreme weather with inadequate clothing, sometimes dodging seeping water from walls and roofs, isn't an adventure," said Dr. Nestor.

"Now that I've interacted with people who don't even have any wall or roof, I understand poverty better."

"There will always remain a difference between understanding poverty and living poorly. When you can choose your fear, it is called adventure. For the poor, fearing for basic survival needs is a habit that is inculcated in them from the moment they are born. A life of provision and a life of deprivation can never comprehend each other fully. They think differently and they act differently."

"You might be more knowledgeable in terms of spending

your childhood in poverty. But as an outsider, I have the benefit of objectivity," Dr. Spunk retorted.

"That's why I let you accompany me, dear Spunk," said Dr. Nestor. He smiled and then turned towards Mr. Candid and Mrs. Bountiful.

"My partner's adventurous spirit and his fixation with fungi converted my place of worship to my work field. Because of him, diseases affecting the poor are in vogue among the scientific community and I will always be grateful to him for that," Dr. Nestor explained.

Junior Mrs. Bountiful translated the discussion between the pilgrim and the adventurer for Mr. Candid. He smiled and halted after a few strides.

"Will you be able to cross a narrow lane with a drain running in the middle of it?" Mr. Candid asked her.

As per their discussion, the fungal experts are good at slum-strolling. Being a novice, however, did not deter Junior Mrs. Bountiful from going ahead with the team.

Mr. Candid entered a one-arm-wide passage that was bordered by walls on both sides. There was an opening on each wall and a young couple was engaged in a passionate criss-cross through these openings.

Mr. Candid continued his march, compelling the young lovers to disengage. While they were hastily arranging their clothes, the two researchers followed their tour guide without any reservation. Junior Mrs. Bountiful was appalled at the thought of entering someone's house without seeking the owner's permission. Poverty could not be an excuse for breaching privacy.

"It's a public lane, Ma'am, not a lobby of a house. They're not husband and wife but indulgent neighbours," said Mr. Candid after realising the lady's dilemma. "If they aren't bothered, why should you bother?"

Once Junior Mrs. Bountiful stepped inside, she realised that the passage she mistook for a house was indeed a narrow lane with a drain running through its middle. Mr. Candid was walking in front of them with each foot on either side of the drain. The lady imitated his style of walking, taking care that her clothes did not rub against the walls.

They were walking in a single file while people from the opposite direction were waiting for them to come out of the lane. Junior Mrs. Bountiful managed to save her dress and reached a reasonably wide brick road. People were talking, laughing and going about their daily chores. They did not look as miserable as underprivileged people should and this surprised the rich lady.

Amid the clusters of rickety dwellings, a few houses caught her attention. There was a small stretch of concrete road running along these houses, which were bigger and had robust and well-finished walls.

"These people are decidedly not poor and can shift to other parts of the city," remarked Mrs. Bountiful.

"Success and prosperity are useful when you can show it off to your family and friends," quipped Mr. Candid.

"But they can at least help in keeping the surrounding clean," said the rich lady.

"Ma'am, there's a dumpyard adjacent to this slum and its residents are accustomed to its ugly sight and stench. If they too get used to cleanliness, where would the city waste go?" Mr. Candid asked.

Without waiting for the lady's reply, he led the team to a vast quarry, half of which is filled with waste and the remaining half was deep and soggy.

"This quarry receives only burnt waste and no organics. Fungi can't thrive in this kind of waste," observed Dr. Spunk. "Miss Axe Effect has made some mistake in sending us here."

"I don't think Miss Effect can make this kind of mistake," said Dr. Nestor.

Junior Mrs. Bountiful connected to Axe over the phone to clear the doubt.

"Treat your visit to Shoddy Slum as an acclimatization to the world of poverty and filth. The slum adjacent to the municipal dumpyard is lot more pathetic and you might find it repulsive. Do you think you can go there?" asked Miss Axe.

The young Bountiful considered these words for a brief moment and replied, "Yes."

Chapter 4

Shifting Objective

There was no open drain built in the middle of a lane or anywhere else in Muck Mound Slum. Sewage exercised its free will, romancing the dusty street and resting in its pits. With their years of experience, Dr. Spunk and Dr. Nestor were at ease in navigating the tricky streets. The rich Bountiful lady also came to terms with her current surrounding sooner than expected.

Abandoned pieces of tattered gunny sacks, tarpaulin, battered wooden boards and metal sheets are enough to build a roof and walls of a house. Cooking, washing utensils and laundry do not need much space if you do not have enough to cook and wear. One can easily carry out these tasks even in the middle of a street and, while doing so, the younger kids can play on the same street in front of your eyes. When you do not fret about cleanliness and orderliness, many other concerns take a back seat. Junior Mrs. Bountiful had a lot to learn during this tour.

The majority of residents were waste-pickers and most of the families had gone out for work. Mr. Candid stopped a few times for conversations with people puttering around and unfailingly introduced his three companions. He lived at Muck Mound Slum and, being a waste contractor, he was a person of prominence. His house, too, was bigger and was constructed of loose bricks instead of discarded wooden boards or metal sheets. The brick walls were not plastered from the outside. Nevertheless, it was distinctively superior to the other neighbourhood dwellings.

The area occupied by the Bountiful house was almost equal to the whole Muck Mound Slum. While Junior Mrs. Bountiful's house was one of the most opulent houses in Dupli City, this slum was one of the poorest settlements. This observation disturbed her. Poverty was much more distressing than she imagined.

The videography team was doing a great job of capturing every moment of the trip. In Shoddy Slum, they could install their equipment in advance. But their itinerary did not mention Muck Mound Slum. They were, however, competent with their job.

Now everyone was on a broad road outside the slum and were walking towards a hillock.

"You have to spend money to go to hill stations and we have a hill in our backyard," said Mr. Candid making a feeble attempt at humour. "We play treasure hunt in the urban mountains of garbage to earn our living."

"I thought you were a waste contractor who collects waste from residential colonies," intervened Mrs. Bountiful. She was not translating her present conversation because the expert duo was busy inspecting the dump site. Dr. Spunk and Dr. Nestor were satisfied with the kind of waste available at the site and the poor living conditions at Muck Mound slum.

Mr. Candid continued talking to Junior Mrs. Bountiful.

"The Municipal Authority of Dupli City (MAD) allowed private companies to filter and take away most of the valuable waste from dumpyards. After a day-long search, waste-pickers could only find a few iron scraps and a minuscule quantity of other useful items. Therefore, we diversified our work and started collecting waste from colonies," he said. "But now, the MAD has invited private companies for waste collection as well."

Mr. Candid pointed out a group of waste-pickers who were

combing the freshly dumped garbage.

"Look at their near-empty sacks after hours of expedition,' he observed.

One of the waste-pickers was a girl of around ten years of age. She was holding an infant while shooing away a dog with her sack. Blood was oozing out of the infant's foot and the sight was nauseating.

"I think I will soon change my job and become a tour guide to show people what poverty looks like because waste may disappear for us, but poverty won't," Mr. Candid said, laughing aloud at his self-deprecating joke before crying bitterly.

Mrs. Bountiful kept him company with a heart-wrenching howl. "My baby! My baby!" she exclaimed.

The suddenness of death, like getting crushed under a rolling garbage mountain, becomes a piece of news. When someone is killed bit by bit, his or her death is qualified as a natural death. Dogs bite waste-pickers, microorganisms feed on their malnourished bodies and pollutants poison them. These are normal occurrences and do not become news. However, a rich lady visiting and witnessing it was certainly a rarity.

The tour video had gone viral. It was incessantly played on news channels and social media. People were going gaga over Junior Mrs. Bountiful. Her excruciating cry for a poor baby suffering a dog-bite had touched many hearts. There were multiple reasons to draw people's attention towards her—youth, glamour and affluence—apart from her heart of gold. But the lady did not speak since her return from the tour as if she had lost her child once again.

The injured baby was admitted into a hospital. All relevant pathological tests were carried out and antibiotics were given along with sugar level management and treatment for anaemia. The baby gradually gained weight.

Apart from being a prudent businesswoman, Senior Mrs. Bountiful was a charitable lady. Without wasting any time, she summoned an NGO working for waste-pickers and expressed her desire to contribute towards their betterment. She brought specific attention towards the girl and the baby in her arms who brought tears to her daughter-in-law's eyes. She bore the expense of the baby's medical care and the ten-year-old girl was admitted to a school. Their nutritional needs and education till their graduation would be sponsored by the elder Bountiful lady, and later, based on their qualification, they would be employed in one of their companies.

Her benevolence, coupled with her daughter-in-law's empathy, was drawing more and more customers for Bountiful products. My employer waited for her daughter-in-law to regain her composure. She wanted to plan a few social events with the young lady to escalate the sales further. Junior Mrs. Bountiful, however, was filled with doubts.

* * *

There were incoherent questions and thoughts scribbled on the whiteboard in the study room. To accommodate Junior Mrs. Bountiful's incessant flow of questions, counter-questions, introspection and speculations, more whiteboards were arranged in the room. These boards were also full and the lady decided to arrange her thoughts within the available writing space.

After a few days of phrasing and rephrasing, young Mrs. Bountiful put together the following points on a single board:

Is waste so precious that government and private firms are trying to snatch it away from poor waste-pickers?

Are waste-pickers shirking, and even denying, waste hazards for fear of losing their livelihood?

Waste-pickers could build their houses from waste and find usefulness in every material that we throw away. Have they acquired better knowledge of waste utilization with years of experience and a paucity of resources?

What can I do for the well-being of waste-pickers apart from charity?

Finding treatment for Callousa Attapata will be beneficial for its patients and it also might turn out to be profitable for our pharmaceutical business. But what is my role in its research?

* * *

The day after formalizing her doubts, Junior Mrs. Bountiful reached Miss Axe Effect's office.

"Apart from their expertise in fungi, Dr. Spunk and Dr. Nestor have considerable knowledge of poverty, waste and waste-pickers. We can seek their assistance in finding a workable solution for waste-pickers' benefit," suggested young Mrs. Bountiful.

"These two fungal experts are sensitive souls and like to work for the poor. But their obsession with poverty is so great that they would prefer to preserve it rather than assist in its eradication," reasoned Miss Axe.

She was busy scribbling something on a notepad while conversing with Mrs. Bountiful. "Wait for a few more days. People will find a new viral video on social media and then no one will trouble you to act like a Messiah," she said.

Junior Mrs. Bountiful kept quiet.

"If you still wish to do something, pick up a less distressing problem."

"I did not pick any problem to showcase empathy or become

a Messiah. If you've forgotten, let me remind you that it was your suggestion to visit the slums with those researchers. It was your job to keep an eye on them, but you set me for the task and loaded my head with this problem," said Junior Mrs. Bountiful, vexed by Miss Axe Effect's suggestions.

The lady detective refused to buckle under her rich client's vexation and said, "You wished to receive the minutest details of this case."

There was another moment of silence before Mrs. Bountiful spoke.

"It was my bad luck that such a scene unfolded in front of me."

"Dog bite is a professional hazard that these people have learned to live with. Mr. Candid was not crying over that. Instead, he was distressed over his diminished source of livelihood and the prospect of losing it entirely," explained Miss Axe objectively. "Try to focus on your business. In a few days, the impact of what you have seen will fade away and you will be at ease."

Junior Mrs. Bountiful blinked as her eyes adjusted to look at Miss Axe Effect. Both ladies were trying to read each other's thoughts.

* * *

Junior Mrs. Bountiful came back from Miss Axe Effect's office and was packing her luggage. Her target was to fit her clothes, shoes, accessories, toiletries, cosmetics and medications in a single suitcase. After many attempts, it seemed an impossible task. One of her immediate staff was worried that exasperation may set in. He hinted at changing the size of the suitcase. The lady took up the suggestion and met her target of fitting her belongings into a single piece of baggage.

The young lady left with a big suitcase. She maintained her

silence but dropped a handwritten note for her husband. The note read: "I am in search of a few answers. Please excuse my absence."

Junior Mrs. Bountiful had shifted to the homely cabins of Miss Axe Effect's office. Clauses of the rent agreement indicated that she could stay there for a few weeks. Junior Mrs. Bountiful had not only imposed a prolonged absence on her husband but also debarred him from visiting her. This debarment had stripped Mr. Bountiful of the opportunity of a chance meeting with Miss Effect.

Although I would have preferred the young lady to find her answers from the comfort of her familial home, I supported her in eliminating the possibility of interaction between her husband and the pretty detective. Sentimentality is a good thing, but one must practice trust only as far as it doesn't jeopardize one's interest.

Junior Mrs. Bountiful also understood that the homely office cabins could not provide her emotional comfort. That's why she took her three-year-old daughter along with her. However, on her husband's insistence, an arrangement was made. According to this arrangement, Baby Bountiful would spend the daytime at her family home and nighttime with her mother.

Senior Mrs. Bountiful was a lady who had never let anything deter her from performing her duties, be it personal, professional or social. Concern for her son and his wife had led her to remain in touch with Mr. Peeptown. There was no restriction on his visit to the detective's office and once again, he proved to be a dependable gentleman.

Mr. Peeptown eased Senior Mrs. Bountiful's worries and the lady paid complete attention to the information he shared.

* * *

Back at the new accommodation, Junior Mrs. Bountiful tacked

multiple layers of newspapers and magazine cuttings on a soft-board. She immersed herself in the pool of knowledge to understand waste and the problems associated with its management. To find a viable and long-lasting solution for the betterment of waste-pickers, she had committed to toil hard. There were also bookmarked online articles to assist in her quest to find solace. The injured baby had exacerbated her grief of child loss and she was in urgent need of relief.

What kind of waste goes into dumpyards and in what proportion? There were numerous papers dispensing this data without much variation. However, there was disagreement over the amount and proportion of waste that is recycled, composted, landfilled or openly dumped. Environmental activists also pointed out that waste collection and disposal from a few model localities were cited as an example of successful waste management while poor localities continued receiving piles of mixed waste.

Other social activists joined the chorus and raised their voices against Waste Racism—a system in which the poorest had to bear the burden of the overindulgence of the wealthy. They proposed a policy of taxation on rich waste generators to create a health cess for the poorest who are facing the adverse effects of deteriorated air and groundwater quality due to gaseous pollutants and leachate emitted from solid waste. However, no one sought relocation of the slums away from landfills.

There was a set of news clippings regarding waste import. Financially constrained countries imported paper, cotton, iron or plastic waste according to their domestic manufacturing demands. Exporting countries believed that if benign waste can be sent, there was no harm in sending hazardous waste as well. After all, when importing countries were benefiting from rich countries' waste, who else would bear the burden of ill effects of their waste? Environmental activists, however, found this positioning exploitative and called it Waste Colonialism.

Over the years, few of these waste-importing countries had grown financially and could generate enough waste domestically to sustain their manufacturing and recycling industry. Therefore, these better-off countries had either banned or were in process of banning waste import. With financial betterment, the previous importers of waste were no longer ignoring the hazards associated with their recycling practices. Public health and environment protection were now receiving due attention in these countries.

Developed countries too were setting up recycling infrastructure in their own backyards and some of them were even moving towards banning the export of waste. Every country was acting according to their circumstances, yet, none failed to boast about its green virtuousness.

Grandstanding seldom solves anything. So, as expected, green virtuousness failed to eliminate waste colonialism. Poorer countries still existed and they carried on treating exported waste as an asset. Even in countries where a ban was in place, the legal deals were merely replaced by illegal transactions. Many rich countries were also happy with this arrangement because they were generating more waste than they could recycle or reprocess. The game of exploiting and getting exploited continued. Only rules and players were changing.

Contradictions and one-upmanship did not stop here. It spilled into every other information related to waste. Plastic being a headline grabber among waste warriors, Junior Mrs. Bountiful read about it in detail.

Plastic has strong resilience to withstand half-hearted bans or the negative propaganda that has been carried out against it for many years. From automobiles to kitchen appliances, the most complicated medical equipment to a modest syringe, disposables that are used not just for convenience but hygiene and increasing shelf-life of food and beverages—plastic is everywhere. Plastic loyalists are secure in the knowledge that it has no competent replacement in sight. They highlight affordability, ease of use and transportability to emphasize that plastic as a material is not a problem but plastic as a waste, is.

Plastic has flooded the market with cheaper products and invaded even the lives of its most ardent detractors. Junior Mrs. Bountiful gained new knowledge and perspective. Cheaper goods raise more waste by quickening the cycle of purchasing and dumping. On the other hand, high-end products are detrimental because they encourage the destruction of unused goods to protect brand value.

The lady got hold of an article with the headline, Eco-friendly consumerism: Feeling virtuous without giving up immoderation. The article talked about Green Washing, that is, misleading consumers into believing that a company's product is environmentally sustainable. Consumers of such goods do not evaluate or question the actual environmental impact of green-washed products because it is convenient to believe their worthiness. Convenience-driven ignorance was the culprit, the rich lady concluded in her notes.

Junior Mrs. Bountiful also understood why governments made policies, but failed to implement them effectively. Industries promised to be environment friendly but could not go beyond tokenism. Hashtags trend but were not followed by actions. Green-Washing was countered by Green Trolling and the nomenclature got enriched with new terminologies, but the situation remained unchanged on the ground. Even those who wished to act were not able to shed their reluctance to do so. Collectively, we are consuming natural resources at almost double the rate at which earth can regenerate it and, for the first time, man-made things had outweighed living things in the year 2020. Convenience-driven ignorance was the culprit, the lady once again concluded.

* * *

Beautiful fruits and vegetables inspire chefs and cooks to spend hours in their kitchens to prepare fanciful dishes. Junior Mrs. Bountiful too believed that misshapen food items lead to loss of appetite. That's why the term Cosmetic-Food-Wastage led her to a question—Are ugly fruits and vegetables similar to ugly patches in society that we discard even if they are good in terms of nutrition or fruitfulness?

The reminder of ugly patches in society hit her hard and brought her focus back to ending the social obliteration of waste-pickers. Knowledge is limitless and it should not be used as an excuse for inaction. Therefore, Junior Mrs. Bountiful decided to move back to her home and start working. Her first goal was to ensure an uninterrupted supply of waste to Muck Mound Slum so that its waste-pickers could directly use, repurpose or sell it without digging into the hazardous garbage dump.

* * *

While listening to Mr. Peeptown, Senior Mrs. Bountiful realised that he must have been peeping into the cabin of her daughter-in-law and hacking her gadgets to collect these pieces of information. The thought would make her son uncomfortable and, thus, she withheld the details of Junior Mrs. Bountiful's waste explorations from him.

Senior Mrs. Bountiful prepared her son and the staff members for her daughter-in-law's arrival. My employer anticipated the impending changes that Junior Mrs. Bountiful would bring along, but she remained calm and happy.

The young Mrs. Bountiful returned home after more than a month. She had set a new goal—reduction, segregation and repurposing of waste. It was hard to waver her resolve and, at this point in time, the fungus, Callousa Attapata completely lost its battle of gaining attention from a beautifully rich lady.

Chapter 5

Waste Enlightenment

Junior Mrs. Bountiful confined the scope of her experiment to herself and her immediate staff. She did not want to test the patience of her husband and mother-in-law by insisting on their inclusion in the testing of her idea.

There were new connections added to her contact list—waste-pickers, organizational and individual influencers, scholars, administrators and activists—everyone who was associated with waste management was under her radar. Her most frequent calls were made to the waste contractor, Mr. Candid, whom she met during her first trip to the slums.

Two weeks had already passed since the young lady rolled out her experiment and she did not divulge any details. Her secrecy was jeopardising her mother-in-law's plan of social announcements related to her new initiative. Senior Mrs. Bountiful volunteered to become a part of the young lady's minimum-waste lifestyle with immediate effect. She also cajoled her son into doing the same. The daughter-in-law expressed her joy but reminded her loving family that she was still learning.

"Never mind, we'll learn together," said her mother-in-law.

When the owner of the house, along with her whole family committed to doing something, their employees were left with no alternative but to fall into line. Junior Mrs. Bountiful prepared a clear-cut instruction manual for each category of household staff and family members, not giving them time to change their minds. Her personal staff who had already been following the segregation and waste minimisation norms were asked to guide the new participants.

The Bountiful house had a large space demarcated for accommodating their daily trash. A week after the full-fledged waste management experiment began, an altercation occurred at the waste container site.

They were two municipal waste collectors who picked up waste from our locality. Once put in the tipper, the waste becomes a municipal asset and, therefore, the waste collectors would retrieve valuables from Bountiful trash containers before transferring the remaining garbage to the municipal tipper. To earn this exclusive profit, they paid a monthly facilitation fee to one of our janitors. This janitor, in return, allowed them to carry out sorting of waste at Bountiful premises.

For the past week, the two waste collectors were not receiving useful waste from the Bountiful house. They had been accusing the janitor of stealing and selling the waste to someone else despite charging the facilitation fee from them. They could not believe that no saleable waste had been disposed of from the house for an entire week. They repeatedly blamed the janitor for cheating. In retaliation, the janitor called them trash scavengers. The duo took great pride in being treasure hunters and could not take the insult. The matter turned hostile.

I reached the site of altercation after receiving a call from the security staff. Since the matter was related to waste, Junior Mrs. Bountiful was duly informed. The municipal waste collectors tried to escape, but our guards did not let them. The lady urged the duo to tell her more about their work.

The waste collectors had been caught bribing her staff and could not escape the guards. With no other option available, they agreed to divulge the details.

"We're supposed to be employees of the private waste concessionaire appointed by the Municipal Authority of Dupli City (MAD) but the concessionaire doesn't pay us a salary. We have to earn our living by selling waste," said one of the waste collectors. "We are honest and hardworking people, Ma'am. We pick up only those things that are thrown in trash barrels. Moreover, if we transfer valuables to a municipal tipper, it would be mixed with the rest of the filth and either be burnt or end up in a dumpyard."

When the waste collectors hesitated to disclose the items they generally recover, the janitor pitched in to atone for his sin of accepting a bribe. "Used clothes, shoes, toys, appliances and all other items that are either workable or almost workable," he said.

"No one throws workable items," the lady said, rejecting the janitor's statement.

"These items become redundant once they are replaced by their latest substitutes," one of the waste contractors explained.

The lady nodded in agreement and recalled reading about Tech Fashionistas.

"These people aspire to remain ahead in the race of acquiring the latest gadget even if it doesn't have enough utility quotient for them. There also are many Tech Retards who jump into the bandwagon despite having the least knowledge about the intended use of the technology. The underlying motto is, if you have money to buy, you are entitled to own anything new that comes into the market," she said.

Junior Mrs. Bountiful's speech was candid and her demeanour was cordial. She could establish a good rapport with the waste contractors. When she asked them about the difference between a trash scavenger and a treasure hunter, the two waste collectors unanimously decided to provide an honest answer.

"Different types of localities have different waste compositions. Poor people don't have much to throw and the middle-income group is learning to throw away valuable trash. There are only a handful of households in Dupli City that dispose of trash of convenience. Those who get the opportunity to hunt in these treasure troves are known as treasure hunters," one of them answered. "Those who loiter around dumped filth to pick recyclables are called trash scavengers."

Waste-pickers also had a hierarchy and those higher in the hierarchy did not like to be recognized as a lowly scavenger. Junior Mrs. Bountiful was distressed by discrimination.

I wished I could explain to her that discrimination is a convenient concept. To practice genuine equality one would need to give up many comforts and this is a daunting task for human beings. We needed people to carry out our repulsive tasks.

The lady's speech about tech fashionistas reminded me of the role of technology in eliminating slavery to a great extent. Otherwise, most of the menial jobs that were now carried out by machines would still be done by human beings.

A day might come when all menial tasks could be carried out by robots and other machines throughout the globe. Till then, our inconsequential brethren have to bear the burden for the upkeep of the society.

* * *

Sulking over discriminatory tendencies of humankind was set aside in a matter of few minutes and Junior Mrs. Bountiful was back at work.

Senior Mrs. Bountiful encouraged her daughter-in-law to extend the waste experiment to all Bountiful factories, offices and staff residential colonies. A childlike excitement filled Junior Mrs. Bountiful's heart. Mr. Bountiful brought a mug of milk in front of his wife's lips. Her lips touched the mug but she forgot to sip the milk.

Senior Mrs. Bountiful sighed, looking at her son. She had unwittingly upset the equilibrium of his wife's physiological responses.

As soon as the elder lady and her son finished their breakfast, Junior Mrs. Bountiful wiped her daughter's hand and mouth. She summoned the nanny and handed over the child to her. This was her usual routine.

The young lady rushed to her study room to collect some reference material and returned with her bag.

"I am leaving for the office early," said the lady excitedly. "I can't delay in preparing the waste management plan for all the Bountiful premises."

A smile spread on Mr. Bountiful's face. His smile put Senior Mrs. Bountiful at ease because her son was ready to be ignored by his wife for the next few days.

* * *

After due consultation with experts and carrying out waste flow mapping, Junior Mrs. Bountiful proposed an online waste exchange platform. It would indicate the items that are discarded at one premise that could be utilised at another place. With real-time charting, this e-platform would also track utilisation and idle periods of feedstock.

The young lady suggested that if other companies are brought on a waste exchange e-platform, it would be more beneficial for resource optimisation and waste minimisation. However, Senior Mrs. Bountiful countered her proposal by suggesting that they must begin the work as a pilot project at their offices, FMCG and pharmaceutical factories and retail outlets. Once it was streamlined, they might extend it to include others. The daughter-in-law agreed readily.

Junior Mrs. Bountiful looked at her husband and found that he was satisfied with the proceeding. Consequently, she revealed the next step for waste reduction—launching a new range of consumer products with smaller waste footprints. Smiles from the faces of mother and son vanished. The young lady sat down. She was no longer happy.

Even before her marriage, Junior Mrs. Bountiful was keen on the family business. It was only after the illness and demise of her second child that the young lady immersed herself in other matters. From the time she visited the slums and witnessed how rag-pickers had to compete even with dogs for their livelihood, the lady had shifted her focus on waste. I suppose Junior Mrs. Bountiful must be shocked to realize that the life of an inconsequential human being was worse than the life of an animal.

The young lady was taking interest in Bountiful business in a different manner than what she did previously and her husband did not want her to stop. Mr. Bountiful was a man who did not interfere in anyone else's domain. His wife had initiated the waste minimization project with encouragement from his mother. Therefore, he signaled to his mother to take the proceeding further.

"We are waiting for you to share your plans," said the elder lady. She, too, did not want her daughter-in-law to back away and re-acquire her sorrowful disposition.

"I thought none of you are interested," said Junior Mrs. Bountiful.

"You know that I can listen to you for hours," said Mr. Bountiful.

He was a naturally romantic man. His wife blushed but hesitated to speak about her plan.

"I advise you to reserve your lovey-dovey chit-chats for some other time and let's hear from the lady what kind of product range she has considered," the elder lady chipped in.

Her intervention nipped the romantic conversation in the bud. Instead of annoying Junior Mrs. Bountiful, it filled her with renewed enthusiasm.

"Our technical team has assured me that they can produce a powdered form of Bountiful shampoos and liquid soaps in a short period. Initially, it will increase our manufacturing cost but will reduce our packaging and transportation cost," said Junior Mrs. Bountiful. "The end users can easily dilute the powder by adding water in measurable bottles."

"What about lazy end-users?" asked Senior Mrs. Bountiful.

"They can continue using what they are already using."

"So, you're suggesting an additional range of products without replacing our older products?"

Junior Mrs. Bountiful nodded and continued sharing her plans.

"We can also provide a refilling facility for our already available products like shampoo, soaps, cleaners etc. at our retail outlets. People can bring their container and fill it there."

The elder lady agreed to consider the refilling proposal and then asked her daughter-in-law to rein her enthusiasm. There were enough schemes to work on and Sunday lunch was waiting to be laid on the table.

Mr. Bountiful ran his fingers through his daughter's hair. Baby Bountiful did not interrupt her father. But as soon as he removed his hand, she requested her nanny to comb her hair. She did not approve of dishevelled hair at family mealtimes.

Baby's father enjoyed teasing her and Baby's grandmother

adored her elegance. Baby's mother, however, was engrossed in other things and was aloof to such trivialities.

"Mrs. Vain Vanity is supporting the cause of climate crisis for the past few years and she has sworn not to buy clothes and accessories anymore," said Mr. Bountiful while the food was being served.

"In eighty years of her life, she has accumulated enough," said his wife. "Even if she changes her clothes ten times a day, her stock would last beyond her hundredth birthday."

"Fashionistas are supposed to indulge and so did she. But with her current abstinence from purchase, she has established herself as an environmental campaigner," said Mr. Bountiful. "I think we can consider her as the brand ambassador of our upcoming sustainability range."

"I don't think she can inspire youth or even middle-aged people to renounce the life of indulgence by giving up shopping at the age of eighty," Junior Mrs. Bountiful retorted.

"Why do you want to push youngsters towards a frugal life?" Senior Mrs. Bountiful asked her daughter-in-law.

"I'm not pushing anyone towards anything. But I wish the younger generation breaks the shackles of consumerism."

"I don't know what the future generation will do. But, if you carry on with your recently adopted lifestyle, I am afraid your daughter will be discouraged to buy anything at all," said Senior Mrs. Bountiful.

My employer along with her family and staff had joined hands in minimising waste under the guidance of her daughter-in-law. However, everyone was falling short of the yardsticks set by Junior Mrs. Bountiful through her actions. The young lady did not do anything half-heartedly but, this time, she seemed to have gone overboard. She had fixed seven dresses for seven days of a week and these attires are repeated week after week.

"I am not against buying. But we shouldn't buy more than what we can use," said the young lady.

"Are you accusing us of hoarding?" asked the elder lady.

"Check your closets. You'll find many items that haven't been used even once."

The argument was escalating and two equally passionate ladies had not touched their lunch yet. Mr. Bountiful was sure about his non-interference doctrine but unsure about the appropriateness of munching while his co-diners were engaged in an argument. Once his daughter began to eat, however, he found the opportunity to take on his meal. Even the ladies did not seek his attention during their arguments.

"Not only that, we throw these unused or rarely used items when we decide to declutter our closets," the young lady continued. "We burden the earth with our indulgence and the poor pay the price."

"Is it our fault if we are rich?" the elder lady retorted.

"No. But why should poor people bear the burden of our unnecessary accumulation?" questioned the young lady.

The ladies were so refined that an outsider would never realise whether they were exchanging pleasantries or lambasting each other until one heard what was spoken and in what context.

"Instead of trying to solve their problem, you aspire to curtail human temptations, aspirations, and creativity," said Senior Mrs. Bountiful.

"I am not giving up my aspirations, temptations or creativity, but learning to align them differently.," responded the young lady.

"Your benchmark is too stringent for a three-year-old child who has lived a life of unhindered abundance till now," warned her mother-in-law.

"I might encourage my daughter to alter her lifestyle, but will never impose my benchmark on her."

"Still, she'll be confused with two diametrically opposite lifestyles prevailing at home," the elder lady said with a lot of concern. "Don't expect me to diminish my standard of living."

"Let's see who alters and who doesn't," the young lady said, laughing heartily.

There was a long silence after her laugh.

"Why don't you become the brand ambassador of Bountiful Sustainability products?" Mr. Bountiful asked his wife. "You're rich, gorgeous and sufficiently famous. And you also have adopted a minimal lifestyle at such a young age."

"Don't entice her," Senior Mrs. Bountiful reprimanded her son. "With time, sorrow will lose its effect."

"Do you think I need sorrow to adhere to my resolve?" asked Junior Mrs. Bountiful.

"I fear that creating a public image will compel you to stick to your resolve. I'm trying to save you from that compulsion."

The young lady took a sip of water.

"I will be the brand ambassador," she announced.

When the elder lady asked whether she was sure, she nodded confidently.

Chapter 6

Setbacks

The launch of the waste exchange e-platform and green products range was many weeks away. Meanwhile, a few popular waste management tricks were rolled out at all Bountiful offices, factories and residential complexes. These include discouraging disposables and encouraging waste segregation, reduction and reuse.

A site was designated inside each complex for composting and collection of dry waste. A board enlisting waste segregation guidelines and other solid waste management instructions were fixed at each site. To eliminate doubts, workshops were conducted.

Junior Mrs. Bountiful held a general meeting for all the employees and their family members to seek their active support. There were a few people with visible worry lines and a few others who openly displayed their enthusiasm. However, the majority constituted of people with expressionless faces.

The worried lot was ignorant about the methods of waste minimization but keen to join the solid waste management campaign. The enthusiastic lot was aware as well as keen to participate in the campaign. However, the majority were neither aware nor keen to play a role. For them, the employer's will mattered the most.

* * *

Under the waste minimisation programme, a Credit Point System was introduced to incentivise optimum utilization of office inventory. These points would reflect in the Bountiful employees' annual assessment reports. Simultaneously, Community Asset Banks were formed at all Bountiful residential complexes. The purpose of Community Asset Bank was to stock household items that were used sporadically and Junior Mrs. Bountiful registered herself as a member to motivate others.

"Today, as a member of Community Asset Bank, I pledge not to buy occasionally used items," announced the young lady. "Our collective assets will be very helpful in saving the earth's resources. It will also declutter our houses, save money and help in developing a sense of community among us."

A huge cheer arose from her audience. Most of the people, however, did not care about saving anything else but their own money. Those who did not have sensitivity, either towards the environment or money, were sulking. They lacked the zeal to join the crusade against waste. They also lacked the courage to ask the question—when the whole world is dumping waste, why were they dissuaded from doing so?

I was a resident of one of the Bountiful residential colonies that were maintained exclusively for Bountiful employees. Reduce, Reuse, Reprocess/Recycle was the waste management mantra. While working as the Chief Security Officer of the Bountiful family, I was exposed to these processes and I had no qualms following these fanciful tricks. It was a part of my job and I was a dutiful employee. However, in my personal life, the idea of involving everyone in waste management did not delight me. I was a firm believer in the principle of division of work. It made people more skillful and efficient in the specialised task that was assigned to them.

* * *

The dog-bitten baby and Mr. Candid's cry still lingered in Junior Mrs. Bountiful's memory. Her waste enlightenment journey began at Muck Mound Slum and as a tribute of gratitude, her waste management initiatives were directed at one goal—to make life better for the people at Muck Mound Slum.

The surroundings of the slum dwellers were diminished and distorted. The walls of their houses were rickety as if they were either deformed due to malnutrition or crumbling under excessive load. Water did not hesitate to seep into them and wind liked to blow them away. Drains in their neighbourhood did not bother to follow a fixed path. Besides distorting their surroundings, the burden of poverty also misshapened the poor's dreams, physique, thoughts and tenderness of emotions. Passersby cringed their noses and faces when they came across these decrepit people and their surroundings.

Junior Mrs. Bountiful could simply provide the funds for their uplift. However, she wanted the waste-pickers of Muck Mound Slum to work with her towards their betterment. To train, organise and keep them motivated, she had to visit the slum every workday. She required an office-cum-workshop to ensure her regular presence.

As soon as the location was finalised, another matter popped up—the living conditions of the slum. Before building an office and workshop, the sanitary condition of the area had to be taken care of. The people in the slum were used to living in filth but Junior Mrs. Bountiful was not.

The rich lady surveyed Muck Mound Slum once again with Mr. Candid, the waste contractor. Mr. Candid understood her dilemma.

"It is difficult to clean this place and to keep it clean afterwards will be even more difficult," said the waste contractor.

"Then what do you suggest?"

"If you are willing to help, I promise you my full support."

His expression was a mixture of doubt, hope and keenness to change the fate of the slum. Junior Mrs. Bountiful expressed excitement for the task and Mr. Candid's disclaimer that he was a man of limited means and skills did not dampen her spirit.

On her next visit to Muck Mound Slum, the lady was accompanied by one of the engineering consultants who planned Bountiful offices and residential complexes. Working in a challenging locality excited the engineer. He started measuring surface elevations to design an improvised sewerage system. The inconsistent slopes confused him, but he did not give up. In a few days, he came up with a layout plan of drains to contain the free-flowing sewage without causing inconvenience to the residents of the thickly packed houses.

While drains and office-cum-workshop were constructed, Junior Mrs. Bountiful felt the need to refurbish the houses of the slum-dwellers. She believed that better surroundings would result in better work efficiency. Moreover, a little cleanliness was not harmful to anyone.

The young Mrs. Bountiful met a few popular architects. But each one of them was keen to showcase their unique designs. After years of impressing people with their environmentally fashionable materials and designs, they were unable to accept that there would not be any extravagant upgradation.

Where there is a will, there is a way. The enthusiastic lady found an unknown architect who could use reclaimed material and the art of minimalism to refurbish low cost houses. He was also willing to utilise materials that were already available with the slum dwellers.

Mr. Candid might be a man of limited resources. But he was resourceful in his work-field. He knew the sources of all sorts of reclaimed material. Under the guidance of the architect and the engineer, he assisted in the procurement of suitable materials at the lowest price. He also motivated the slum dwellers to commit a few hours of labour for the remodelling of the slum. As his trust in Junior Mrs. Bountiful was growing, so was his helpfulness.

Junior Mrs. Bountiful began interacting with other slum dwellers during the revamping work. She shared her plan to hire a craft teacher who could teach toy-making using discarded waste. Waste-pickers listened to her, but neither agreed to, nor declined, her proposal.

"You don't have to pay to learn," she told them.

It brought a smile on most of the faces of her audience.

"We'll sell the toys made by you and you'll get your share of the profit," she added.

Their smiles got broader.

* * *

A craft teacher was appointed for Muck Mound Slum dwellers. Junior Mrs. Bountiful set up waste collection centres at the Bountiful premises without any delay and the collected waste was supplied to the newly toy-makers of the slum. Their finished toys would be sold back only at Bountiful colonies before bringing them to market.

Many times, if one has to wait for success, nagging self-doubt shakes one's resolve and perseverance. Thankfully, Junior Mrs. Bountiful found early adulation. The young lady's multi-pronged efforts at factories, offices, residential colonies and Muck Mound Slum were well received by the general public and netizens. Bountiful companies saw substantial growth in the past year and Junior Mrs. Bountiful got most of the credit for giving a new direction to the Bountiful business.

If you could use mass media tools to propel your honour and fame, someone else could use the same tools to tarnish your reputation. As soon as the launch date of Bountiful Sustainable Range was announced, their waste management initiatives started receiving brickbats. Memes, videos, printed articles and various other public forums projected the Bountifuls as eco hypocrites. The Bountiful daughter-in-law was particularly projected as a hoodwinking waste crusader. Protests were organized outside all Bountiful premises. However, Muck Mound slum was spared from this slander campaign.

It was clearly a well-planned campaign to malign Bountiful's upcoming sustainable product range. I would not go into the details of who had been conspiring against my employer's family. Propaganda and counter-propaganda were part and parcel of businesses.

The underlying allegations of the counter-campaign were malpractices in composting and waste segregation at Bountiful premises, stealthy disposal of toys made by waste-pickers, deceptive waste credit points and unworkable Community Asset Banks. Junior Mrs. Bountiful could not believe that she and her family were accused of such petty things.

Disbelief in allegations was replaced by doubts during the course of the night—her intention was not to cheat, but had she failed to implement what she intended? Instead of relying on officially submitted reports, Junior Mrs. Bountiful decided to visit each of the Bountiful premises in Dupli City to verify the factuality of these accusations.

Bountiful employees and their families had to segregate waste. They were expected to carry it out as a daily ritual during their office hours and within their familial space. However, when employees got an option to please their employer through good results instead of the correct process, they opted for easily attained results and gave up a cumbersome process.

Collecting compostable waste and then waiting for it to become manure required effort and patience. Unwilling or unaware minds lack both. Readymade compost was procured from the market to earn Junior Mrs. Bountiful's appreciation during her visits, which were few and far in between. This time, the upset lady caught them unawares and discovered the reality.

She also noticed dust-ridden items on the racks of the Community Asset Bank that revealed their unused status. There was no entry made in the transaction register after her last visit. It indicated that previous entries were fudged and these items were not issued to the residents of Bountiful Complex.

Along with fudged entries and dust-ridden items in the Community Asset Bank storage, Junior Mrs. Bountiful found out that toys purchased from the waste-pickers had been dumped in a corner. Bountiful employees were treating these purchases as a part of taxation on their salary. They were buying these toys only to please their employer and were unwilling to let their kids play with them.

Junior Mrs. Bountiful did not say a word. She got the toys packed and sent them to Muck Mound Slum.

I admit that I was one of the covert supporters of these alternative arrangements of composting, dumping of waste-toys and even fudging the Community Asset Bank register at our residential complex. But this was before I realised its ill-effects on my employers' reputation. Likewise, most of the residents must have opted for it because of convenience without intending ill for the Bountiful family.

* * *

At the lunch table, Junior Mrs. Bountiful fed her child and hurriedly finished her meal. She had also taken it upon herself to put her daughter to sleep. Once done, she left her sleeping child under the nanny's supervision and reached the head office.

The lady did not take long to understand that the story of

composting was repeating here. She called the waste management in-charge, Mr. Mender to enquire about the procurement of manure from market.

"Unfavourable weather, unsegregated waste, and wrong methodology failed my attempt to compost. To hide my failure, I procured ready-made compost," confessed Mr. Mender. "I extended this deception to residential colonies as well."

He also confessed that he was disposing of official documents without entering them in the waste disposal datasheet so that Bountiful employees could earn Waste Credit points.

Waste Credit points were allotted based on saving office inventory. Employees were supposed to print on both sides of the paper but they were habitually printing single-side. To correct their mistake, they were reprinting the documents. Mr. Mender was selling off the discarded one-side printed documents to a paper recycler to cover up their mistake.

On further enquiry, Junior Mrs. Bountiful was told that the recycler shredded the documents in front of the heads of the concerned departments to safeguard confidentiality.

"Your methods might look devious, but your intentions are not," the lady said, with a hint of a smile on her face. "You ensured confidentiality of official documents while helping out your colleagues."

* * *

Mr. Mender and I stayed in adjacent blocks at one of the Bountiful residential complexes. Like everyone else, he too did not anticipate the slandering of the Bountiful family over social media. Nevertheless, he had a few, partly good news for Junior Mrs. Bountiful:

Bountiful employees were developing a habit of printing on both sides of papers and were also saving other office inventory.

Some of the residents were segregating waste.

In all likelihood, his composting experiments would soon bring a good result.

After a few initial glitches, the Waste Exchange e-platform was functioning well. Once factory employees would get accustomed to this platform, they could expect to fulfil the young lady's dream to promote the waste management mantra—reduce, reuse, refurbish, remodel, recycle and reciprocate. This system would also help in minimizing and scientific disposal of their pharmaceutical waste.

Each problem noticed at the head office seemed to have a solution. But it could not be denied that all of them required attention. If they were not attended to, everything would come to a nought.

Keeping this in mind, Junior Mrs. Bountiful sought an audience with her husband and mother-in-law to apprise them of the situation. She also had to discuss the postponement of the launch of their sustainable product range and refilling facility at their retail stores. Junior Mrs. Bountiful had assented to become the brand ambassador of Bountiful Sustainable Range and, in present circumstances, it would reflect poorly on her as well as on Bountiful company.

"If we defer the launch date or change the brand ambassador at the last moment, it would be even more embarrassing and have adverse effects on our company," reasoned Mr. Bountiful.

There was no discussion on this matter because his wife was convinced of his reason. But she was not as chirpy as she had been in the past months. On the contrary, lines of gloom had begun to appear in the corners of her eyes and lips.

"Teething problems shouldn't discourage us," said her husband.

"You told us, just now, that things were getting streamlined at the office."

"Things are getting better at the office, but I don't know how to make Toys-from-Waste project viable," said his wife. "The entire waste project would be ineffective if it isn't financially sustainable for the waste-pickers."

"I am glad you understand the financial sustainability aspect."

Junior Mrs. Bountiful remained silent. It was clear that the last statement made by her husband had unnerved her. She could not think of a strategy to make waste management a profitable project for waste-pickers. She was not sure of how to convince people to buy these toys for their kids when her family was not letting her little daughter play with them. The same line of reasoning applied to the Community Asset Banks. She had not yet found the courage to bring anything from the bank to use at her house parties, fearing their guests might find it offensive.

* * *

Her waste management projects were lying in tatters. Junior Mrs. Bountiful felt hesitant about becoming the brand ambassador of sustainable products. She, however, fulfilled her commitment as the representative of Bountiful Sustainable Range.

After coming back from the launch, she spent a lot of time in her study room. White and soft boards in the room were overburdened with the flow of information getting written or pinned on them. Junior Mrs. Bountiful she had procured these boards through Mr. Candid, the waste contractor from Muck Mound Slum.

The lady considered talking to a few researchers and academicians who were experts in solid waste management. However, after realising that it would be difficult to explain real-world issues to them, she dropped the idea. With each discarding of ideas, her sadness mounted. The presence of her daughter brought sporadic cheer and she tried to keep her anxiety under wraps.

Meanwhile, her husband and mother-in-law were busy streamlining and expanding the new sustainability projects at Bountiful companies. After many days, the three adult Bountifuls sat together.

"You are deviating from your goals," said Senior Mrs. Bountiful.

"I want to find a way out, but I don't know how," the young lady confessed.

Anxiety is now visible on her face.

"You can never begin anything from perfection," said Senior Mrs. Bountiful. "Learn to convert criticism into growth and do what you consider best."

Junior Mrs. Bountiful was not willing to receive any advice. She was tempted to go back to her study room and resume stacking information on her boards. But before she could leave, her husband intervened.

"Work, work and work. Nothing else, but mistakes can bring clarity at this moment," he said.

"What should I work on?" asked the lady.

"Correcting the mistakes that have occurred," her husband told her.

"When our employees aren't keen, how can I expect strangers to support this cause?"

"Support? What kind of support are you seeking from them? Just because they are working in our companies, they aren't bound to align their passion with everything that we do," said Mr. Bountiful. "I have been putting in all my efforts to make your dream products a big success and you are finding excuses to back out."

"You are putting in effort to reap profits. You are neither bothered about my integrity being questioned nor about my dreams getting trampled."

"You weren't the only one who was insulted; our whole family was. But I chose to work harder instead of giving up," countered Mr. Bountiful. "Yes, I like to run a profitable business so that someone can afford to whine and fail to honour her own goals."

"Enough," declared Senior Mrs. Bountiful.

This was the first time the staff witnessed unambiguous acrimony between the husband and wife. However, both of them had the decency to respect the intervention of the elder of the house. Junior Mrs. Bountiful hugged her mother-in-law and cried for a long time. Meanwhile, her husband left the room so that those tears did not melt his heart.

* * *

"I want my daughter to lead a comfortable life," said the husband.

"I, too, want the same, but the definition of comfort is highly subjective," responded the wife.

"Let's keep aside materialistic comforts. You aren't even sure about your plans. Isn't it too early for our daughter to get exposed to the confusion of life?"

"Is confusion a bad thing?"

"No. But it's demanding."

"It is. But, trust me, I am not irresponsible and I will take care of our child in the best possible way."

"Sweetheart, sweetheart! I don't doubt it," said Mr. Bountiful embracing his wife. "Please understand, I don't want to stay away from any of you."

"Everything has come to a standstill and if it continues like this, I will stagnate and sink."

"Okay, fine. Nights yours, days mine," Mr. Bountiful said, proposing an arrangement of dividing their time with Baby Bountiful.

It was the same arrangement that the couple followed during Junior Mrs. Bountiful's month-long stay at Miss Axe's office.

"One week with you and one with me," said Junior Mrs. Bountiful. "If Baby does not like staying with me at Muck Mound Slum, she can continue staying here with you and mom. I will come to meet her."

Mr. Bountiful was speechless. It looked as though his wife was leaving home for a long duration that might extend to many months.

Chapter 7

Her World Falls Apart

Junior Mrs. Bountiful was not able to sleep despite being sleepy. She had landed at Muck Mound Slum alone. Her mother-in-law had vetoed Baby Bountiful's stay at the slum.

Muck Mound was upgraded with the young lady's efforts and it could no longer be classified as an impoverished slum except for the mountain of garbage adjacent to it. However, Senior Mrs. Bountiful was not ready to subject her granddaughter to the stink and sight of the garbage just because her daughter-in-law chose to live there and her son had agreed to the parental time-sharing schedule with his wife.

After upgradation, the slum became better than its previous state, but it still remained a slum. Mr. Bountiful was unwilling to keep his word after witnessing the condition and supported his mother's veto. Surprisingly, even his wife readily agreed with their decision and seemed relieved with the arrangement.

"Let me first make the place suitable for my daughter's stay," she said, expressing her willingness to abide by the elder lady's veto.

The waste-to-toys project had been put on hold. The workshop floor was filled with input goods and toys that could not be sold. The young lady hoped to resolve the issues hampering her waste-to-toys project. Her hope has brought her to Muck Mound Slum despite the waste contractor, Mr. Candid's, caution.

"Coming for work here is different from living in this place," the gentleman told the young lady. "Sympathise with us from a distance because proximity breeds disgust."

The lady, however, insisted on shifting here. A portion of the office-cum-workshop adjacent to a bathroom was renovated for Junior Mrs. Bountiful's residence. The young Bountiful was pushing her austerity limits to the extreme. This residence had nothing but four bare walls and one roof. She failed to recognise that luxuries become necessities for someone who is born and brought up in rich surroundings.

Junior Mrs. Bountiful was not staying away from her family for the first time, but this time she felt abandoned. This feeling of estrangement grew because of the challenging condition she chose for herself. Her restlessness kept her awake. On another hand, after a tiring day of shifting and a dose of tranquillizing medicine, her body demanded rest. She was experiencing a war between sleepiness and sleeplessness.

* * *

It was late in the evening when Junior Mrs. Bountiful reached her new abode. Early in the morning, after a sleepless night, she was surrounded by the press. Before the working hours of the day could end, an eviction notice was served by the Municipal Authority of Dupli City (MAD). Not only the office-cum-workshop, but the entire Muck Mound Slum, was constructed on encroached land. Hence, all residents of the slum were directed to vacate the land within a month.

A crowd of slum-dwellers gathered outside the office-cum-workshop.

"The betterment of our life is a ploy to grab this land," a vocal critic of the waste-to-toys project accused the young Bountiful. "Rich people can't be trusted."

"She has come here to live with us, leaving behind the comforts of her family and home," a supporter of the project said, defending the lady.

"Someone who leaves her family and home for strangers certainly has an ulterior motive," said the detractor. "Once evicted, she will go back to her family. Where will you go?"

The detractor was a lean fellow and was better dressed than the other people in the slum. His name was Canny and people suspected that he indulged in unscrupulous practices to support his lifestyle. Presently, no one could answer him. He had a few silent admirers who openly sided with him and proposed to expel Junior Mrs. Bountiful from Muck Mound Slum.

"Shut your filthy mouths," Mr. Candid said.

He raised his clenched fist and walked towards Mr. Canny and his admirers. Mr. Canny looked at him and then faced the slum-dwellers with nonchalance.

"We can get this eviction notice reversed only after she leaves our slum," said Mr. Canny, endorsing the proposal.

"Do you want to keep this lady here and lose your homes?" he asked, this time to incite the crowd.

"No, no, no." There were shouts all around.

Mr. Candid lowered his fist. Junior Mrs. Bountiful came out of the office-cum-workshop and stood facing the crowd. Shouts gave way to silence.

Many residents of the slum were happy with their upgraded living situation and were hoping for further improvement after the arrival of Junior Mrs. Bountiful. Now, threat of losing their homes eclipsed their hope of betterment. Moreover, their hope was already shaken after the failure of the waste-to-toys venture. They were unwilling to doubt the rich lady's intention but could not trust her capabilities. Their shouts and silence reflected their dilemma.

The family of the dog-bitten baby had received Senior Mrs. Bountiful's generosity and Junior Mrs. Bountiful had provided them with good accommodation. Mr. Candid tried to locate the family so that they could speak in favour of the lady. To his utter dismay, none of them could be seen.

"They're sleeping," someone whispered in his ears.

"All of them?" asked Mr. Candid in disbelief.

The person nodded. Mr. Candid rushed to their house and woke up the father of the dog-bitten baby. The father pushed Mr. Candid away without giving up on his sleep. It was only after he received a slap across his face that the man woke up and, realising his mistake, apologised to the waste contractor. He and his family were blissfully ignorant about the eviction notice and accusation faced by Junior Mrs. Bountiful.

"Do you think the young lady is cheating us?" asked Mr. Candid after briefing them about the day's events.

All of them, including the baby, had woken up. They all shook their heads, disapproving the allegation. But when Mr. Candid asked them to come along to defend the lady, they looked at each other without getting up.

"She's a good lady, but she must go back to where she belongs," said the mother of the baby and the father nodded in agreement.

Mr. Candid was horrified. They did not accuse Junior Mrs. Bountiful of any wrongdoing, yet they supported Mr. Canny's proposal to send her away.

"Last night, all of us visited the saintly lady to pay our regards. She spread delicate linen on her fluffy mattresses and insisted we sit on it. We obeyed but couldn't make even the slightest movement lest our heel fissures shred the bedsheet into threads," explained the mother. "After coming home, we did not sleep. We kept washing our feet the whole night but could not remove those thick and hard fissures that are protruding like thorns on our heels."

Mr. Candid had never been in favour of Junior Mrs. Bountiful's stay at Muck Mound Slum. Like the family of dog-bitten baby he, too, believed that the lady did not belong to this place. Despite drastically altering her lifestyle, she could never shed the label of being rich and privileged. Nevertheless, Mr. Candid was restless because of the land-grabbing accusation hurled at the rich lady. He was eager to find a way out to absolve her from the blame. He left the family of the dog-bitten baby and walked towards the office-cum-workshop.

The crowd outside the office-cum-workshop had dispersed. While going towards their homes, the people indulged in conversation and ended up forming various small groups. Each group hushed its voice as soon as Mr. Candid was in sight.

When Mr. Candid reached the office-cum-workshop, he found Mr. Canny lurking around. The waste contractor lost his temper and pushed the latter to the ground. Mr. Canny, however, was used to such assaults and knew how to hit back. He pulled his assaulter's leg and brought him down to the floor. Both of them wrestled on the ground, trying to get the better of each other. None of them made any sound lest they attract anyone's notice. Coincidentally, Junior Mrs. Bountiful came outside.

"What are you doing!" the lady exclaimed, rushing towards the two men.

Her exclamation was hushed as if to maintain the secrecy of the fight. Hearing her, both men stood up and dusted their clothes. Despite his ongoing revolt against the lady, Mr. Canny behaved like a gentleman. He left the place without uttering a foul word against Mr. Candid or the lady.

"You shouldn't have picked up a fight with Canny," said the young lady to Mr. Candid. However, there was an expression of relief and satisfaction on her face. She realised that Mr. Candid still trusted her despite her blunder.

In her zeal to create better work opportunities for the people of Muck Mound Slum, Junior Mrs. Bountiful forgot that the slum existed on an encroached land and administrative approvals from government authorities were required to make the place legitimate. Her blunder brought the residents on the verge of evacuation from their homes and that was why she could not find fault with the accusation of land grabbing levelled against her.

Mr. Candid could not hold back his tears and fell to his knees.

"I should have stopped you from coming here," he said.

"You tried to," replied the lady and smiled through her tears.

"You aren't alone in making this mistake. When we saw the prospect of a better life, none of us bothered to tell you that we are not the owners of this land. We continued to enjoy benefits, but at the time of adversity, everyone absolved themselves of responsibility," said Mr. Candid.

Before he could drown himself in his tears, Mr. Canny reappeared and walked inside the office-cum-workshop. Mr. Candid and Junior Mrs. Bountiful rushed after him. But before they could combat him, Mr. Canny spoke.

Nobody could overhear his conversation with the lady and Mr. Candid. But after his brief visit, Mr. Canny was not seen anywhere near Mrs. Bountiful for a week.

During this week, Junior Mrs. Bountiful tried to go about her work as usual. She had to understand why her waste management project failed but slum dwellers were concerned only about saving their houses. None of them were reporting for work. The lady did her best to gain as much insight as possible despite her dwindling interactions with the slum dwellers.

Mr. Candid had given consistent support to Junior Mrs. Bountiful in analysing the toy-making process and its shortcomings. She also examined various stages of waste management—collecting, transporting, storing and processing—so that she could devise better alternative.

After the upgradation, residents of Muck Mound Slum did not have to spend hours to fetch water or answer a call of nature. But they still have to struggle each day to earn a meal. They were struggling and passing days in fear of losing their houses. In such a precarious situation, a rich lady's persistence to revive a failed project was causing them a lot of frustration.

At the end of the week, while roaming around the slum, Mr. Candid again found many small groups engaged in conversation. None of them hushed their voice and even accused Mr. Candid of servility. The common gist of all these chats reiterated their collective decision—expulsion of the rich intruder and saving the roofs over their heads.

In a time of crisis, the only source of comfort was to find someone to blame for your ordeal. Junior Mrs. Bountiful was not defending herself and, thus, pronounced guilty.

* * *

Mr. Candid told Junior Mrs. Bountiful that he had requested her family, through her security staff, to take her home. While they were talking, a car and a lorry stopped by on the road that was at a short distance from them.

Someone alighted from the car and, by the time he reached Junior Mrs. Bountiful, she regained her composure. She instructed the man to get her belongings packed and moved away to make a phone call.

Then she went inside the office-cum-workshop to collect few documents and wrote a letter. She put the letter in an envelope and handed it over to Mr. Candid.

All heavy items were loaded in the lorry. But due to lack of space, the lady's bed and bedding could not be loaded.

"We're arranging for another lorry," informed the driver.

"Keep it back in my room," Junior Mrs. Bountiful said. "I might come back." There was no bitterness or agony in her voice. Instead, there was a steadiness in her eyes.

The driver of her car opened the door for the lady and waited for her to settle down in her seat. She closed the door and motioned for him to leave. The driver sat in his seat but did not switch on the ignition. Another car arrived and Junior Mrs. Bountiful went to sit in it. Miss Axe Effect, the lady detective, was already sitting in the backseat of that car.

Chapter 8

PARADIGM SHIFT

The next morning, the condition of Muck Mound Slum began to revert to its previous condition. The slum dwellers were pulling down every visible structure that might strip their slum from the list of an impoverished locality. Mr. Canny and Mr. Candid were at loggerheads over the eviction of Junior Mrs. Bountiful. But, to my utter surprise, they were both leading the task of pauperising Muck Mound Slum.

Within a fortnight of the disappearance of the rich lady, Muck Mound Slum regained the empathy of the Municipal Authority of Dupli City (MAD) and the eviction notice was withdrawn. There was one condition, though: the impoverished status quo had to be preserved in the slum and all its residents must stand against anyone who tried to alter it.

* * *

The day Junior Mrs. Bountiful left the slum, Mr. Candid had visited the Bountiful home and discretely asked for Mr. Bountiful. I had seen them exchanging envelopes, but I could not get hold of any other information. The contents of the parcel must have been disturbing. Every staff member who was within visible range of Mr. Bountiful was receiving his ire and the day ended with him shutting himself inside his room.

The next morning, all staff members were summoned. Getting angry was unusual for a gentleman like Mr. Bountiful. He apologised for his temper and sought forgiveness from each of them.

It was a week since Mr. Candid delivered the distressful parcel.

There was a sudden and unexpected change that was noticeable in Mr. Bountiful's demeanour. He was cheerful and did not come home for days. When, he was at home, he could be found indulging in flirtatious talks over the phone. Nobody knew who he was talking to. But these talks were very frequent, giving enough fodder to staff for gossip.

* * *

On another side of the Bountiful world, my father and Mr. Mender were engaging in strange behaviour.

One day, my father called me.

"Stop keeping an eye on personal lives of the Bountiful family members," he instructed.

I was perturbed because poking my nose into their intimate matters had never been my endeavour. My father had willingly handed over the responsibility of security of the Bountiful family to me.

"Were there any complaints from the family?" I asked in a subdued voice.

He patted my shoulder and smiled.

"You're good at your work," he said. "However, the family needs a little more space and you must take care of their needs."

I bowed my head in agreement and respect. I instructed my network of information-gatherers to keep their ears and eyes shut till further notice.

The responsibility of the security of the Bountiful family was given back to my father, who employed new staff for the purpose. My duty was limited to securing the Bountiful house and their official, industrial and residential premises.

If you remember, Mr. Mender and I lived in adjacent blocks

of the same residential colony. Since Junior Mrs. Bountiful had gone incognito, the solid waste management in-charge of Bountiful offices and residential complexes amplified his efforts to improve solid waste management at these premises. Being a sensitive man, Mr. Mender must have held himself responsible for the lady's plight and wanted to salvage her tarnished reputation.

Composting units, Dry Waste Collection Centres, and Community Asset Banks were now functional. Mr. Mender had developed a fun activity-based park and named it Solid Waste Management Learning Centre. He also installed bio-methanation plants to manage waste generated at Bountiful Food & Drink factories. No one knew how he proceeded in this direction without any permission and how he funded the project.

A few more months passed. It seemed as though Mr. Mender had started earning from this venture. Otherwise, no one would have bothered to join hands in an attempt to knock down his project. I did not mind the profitability of the enterprise because I had witnessed his hard work and undiminished devotion to Junior Mrs. Bountiful's cause. But he had done something to ruffle my feathers and I had banned his entry into my household.

Mr. Mender had launched a community composting-cum-kitchen gardening scheme. Volunteers who deposited waste or compost, or devoted time to the upkeep of this community garden, earned credit points. These points could be used in exchange for vegetables and fruits from the garden. My father had enthusiastically jumped into the foray due to the lure of fresh, organic vegetables. I also liked eating freshly grown vegetables until I discovered that it was brought through bartering waste.

Mr. Mender was luring people into unnecessary frugality and my father was trapped in his scheme. Perhaps this was because he belonged to a generation that had lived a life of lesser comfort. Thankfully, my wife came to my rescue. None of us wanted our kids to become misers and we firmly believed that purchasing things with hard-earned money was not sinful. Rather, the purchased items showcased our hard work, fortune and refinement of taste, thereby, discouraging us from slothful living.

The people, who resented Mr. Mender for making profit by using Bountiful resources, formed a group. I did not accompany this group of complainants, nor did I sign their complaint letter. However, I silently wished them success in cutting off Mr. Mender's tentacles that were spreading miserliness in our society.

The complainants submitted their two-page representation to Senior Mrs. Bountiful. The lady patiently read the complaint regarding the misappropriation of Bountiful resources by Mr. Mender and handed it over to her assistant. Then she took a file from the assistant and gave it to one of the representatives of the complainants.

The representative was taken aback. The file contained a detailed report of Mr. Mender's solid waste management initiatives and their successful outcomes. The later pages were signed by the supporters of his solid waste management projects along with umpteen testimonials. Supporters outnumbered the detractors and, consequently, Senior Mrs. Bountiful reserved one of the Bountiful residential blocks for people who were keen to segregate, reduce, reuse and recycle waste.

When Mr. Mender got the whole-hearted support from the residents of the reserved block, he progressed at a faster pace. Within a couple of months, he began trading in compost and garden produce. The credit point scheme was extended to other solid waste management activities like segregation, reusing waste, community usage of resources and so on. Now, these credit points could also be used to purchase Bountiful Sustainable Range or Refillable Products from their mobile vendors or retail stores. The launching of mobile vendors and redemption of credit points for Bountiful products were done with due approval from Senior Mrs. Bountiful.

More residents filed applications for the inclusion of other residential blocks in the solid waste management programmes. People from outside Bountiful colonies also expressed their keenness to join this endeavour. Besides setting up more Waste Collection Centres and Community Asset Banks, it resulted in the extension of community composting-cum-gardening scheme to richer households. Mr. Mender was appointed as the in-charge.

The pride of cultivating their own food was infused in cash-rich people by amplifying their contribution to the well-being of mother earth. The credit point scheme drew people who rejoiced in availing discounts and saving money. None of these people realised that, each day, they were manipulated to give up their present lifestyle and made to believe that they were doing it voluntarily. They refused to buy new things, made alterations to whatever they already had and passed on things that they did not need. They even started sharing their clothes, shoes and accessories so that they could have more variety to satiate their craving without buying umpteen items. All our lives, we had been groomed to refrain from passing on used things as gifts and, all of a sudden, these people had rephrased them as pre-loved items, which rendered our grooming outdated.

It did not stop at that. Policy guidelines for developing nutrition gardens in government-aided schools existed but were not publicised enough. All of a sudden, many non-profit organisations sprung up to assist government-aided schools in Dupli City to develop such gardens. They propagated this idea to such an extent that even non-aided schools included it in their curriculum. Compost was supplied to these schools from Mr. Mender's compost plants.

Most of the people in Dupli City got onto the circular waste bandwagon and those who did not were made to believe that they were living in a primitive age. No one was called names as such, but there was peer pressure due to aggressive propaganda.

Unlike others, I did not bother about being labelled as outdated. Before barring Mr. Mender from my household, I had a talk with him.

"If this world gets buried under waste, I am ready to be buried with it. I will continue to exhibit my materialistic worth as long as I live," I declared.

Even now, I stand by my statement and would remain committed to my treasured values. However, turn of events made me wonder if Mr. Mender was indeed capable enough to generate a solid waste management frenzy at such a fast pace and to such a vast extent.

* * *

Mr. Candid and Mr. Canny were often seen together ever since the eviction notice of Muck Mound Slum had been revoked. Now, they were invited to the Bountiful house. After multiple visits and long discussions, it became clear that Muck Mound Slum was the next focal point of the solid waste management programme. Involvement in the slum had brought many embarrassments for the Bountiful family and yet, the family could not shun it from their lives.

A few damaged, flat wooden carts were arranged and converted into fancy Solid Waste Management (SWM) learning centres. These mobile SWM learning centres proactively approached residential, commercial and institutional complexes to teach quick tricks to reduce, reuse, and segregate waste along with composting and gardening. They were also reaching at all sorts of events, such as marriages, conferences and concerts. Whether people were willing to learn or not was immaterial. The motive was to have them think about

SWM by serving them repeated reminders.

Once waste began appearing in people's daily conversation, the next step was to direct their thoughts for a profitable pursuit. The Waste Phone App was ready and its pilot run was already successful.

Big companies had the money and influence to profit from solid waste management contracts. The Bountiful family along with Mr. Candid and Mr. Canny decided to stay away from challenging the businesses because waste-pickers did not have the expertise of handling contractual and technical solid waste management processes. Instead, a phone app was created to provide a customer-friendly business opportunity for the waste-pickers.

Presently, waste generators were disposing off their waste according to the rules and schedule laid out by the Municipal Authority of Dupli City (MAD) and its waste concessionaires. The phone app service treated waste generators as esteemed customers, allowing them flexible pickup times, accepting their one-off items and even washing their dustbins. Their service included festive cleaning, pre and post-event cleaning, work space cleaning and cleaning of pets and infants' excreta. It was more than a waste generator could ask for and they were happy.

The rapport built through mobile SWM learning centres helped in persuading even the laziest person to practice basic segregation of his or her waste. Do-it-yourself kits were available to encourage people to take up waste reuse, composting and urban farming. The Credit Points Scheme was once again extended and points were credited for selling and buying waste or waste-made products through the phone app.

The space adjacent to office-cum-workshop at Muck Mound slum was now converted into a warehouse-cum-sorting centre for secondary segregation. The waste-pickers' expertise resulted in quick sorting and they sent sanitary waste, domestic hazardous waste, and electronic waste to suitable waste handlers.

To accommodate an increased volume of bio-degradable waste, composting and bio-methanation plants were constructed in areas outside Bountiful premises. Urban gardens were promoted to utilise an increased quantity of compost. There was a huge demand for fully grown potted plants, which was generated through subscription plans, annual maintenance plans and home delivery.

Some of the collected waste was sold to waste-to-toy makers. One of the reasons for the failure of the previous waste-to-toys project was in not recognising the fact that waste collectors were experts in dealing with waste, not in making toys or marketing them. To make amends, craftsmen were enrolled to create local-themed toys and traditional games. Festivals and events-specific toys also made their way into the market. Marketers were deftly using sustainability, pro-poor and culture-friendliness aspects of these toys to draw scores of customers.

Gradually, various types of bulk waste generators and recyclers registered on the Waste Phone App. Recyclers' data and price trends were regularly updated. A database of businesses and people associated with waste-to-product ventures was created. It also included toy-makers. Regular upskilling, engagement with people and effective strategy quickly made the phone app and waste-to-product ventures successful.

Instead of submitting to failure, the Bountiful family and waste-pickers had chosen to turn the tide in their favour.

Chapter 9
THE WASTE DEITY

It had been almost two years since Junior Mrs. Bountiful vanished and, despite my curiosity, I had abstained from tracking down her whereabouts. She was back at Bountiful House and was received by her mother-in-law, husband and daughter as if the separation did not happen.

There was a wedding of a close relative that had acted as a catalyst for Junior Mrs. Bountiful's return. Jewellery sets were displayed on the table, but the young lady did not exhibit any interest in getting a new set.

"I hope you haven't forgotten that we are rich and used to live a life of luxury," reminded Senior Mrs. Bountiful.

"Jewellery does not exhibit opulence, dear mom, but the skin that wears it," quipped her daughter-in-law.

"It'll be devastating to live a life in which we would be considered inconsequential," the elderly lady said with a sigh.

Junior Mrs. Bountiful laughed at the dramatic sigh and got up to hug her mother-in-law. She also kissed the elder lady on the cheek and received a peck on her forehead in return.

"Don't worry, I am determined to increase my relevance and become more consequential," the young lady said.

"I have always visualised you as a successful entrepreneur," Senior Mrs. Bountiful spoke affectionately.

"This isn't true," teased the young lady. "You've been training me to become a good entrepreneur."

"Because I saw potential in you."

"Are you disappointed that your grooming is wasted?"

"You underestimate my observation and grooming skills. Some students learn more than what they're taught and it's quite evident that you've not only found a way to convert waste into fortune, but you'll soon establish a waste empire."

* * *

The next day, Junior Mrs. Bountiful gave me a big parcel that had to be handed over to my father. I did the needful without expecting my father to reveal the contents of the parcel.

It became clear that the Bountiful family was in touch with the young lady during her time away. My father was also kept in the loop and he aided Mr. Mender to carry out the lady's instructions. Junior Mrs. Bountiful was the real garbage guzzler, not Mr. Mender. I could ban his entry into my home, but how could I avoid my employer or her family members? Did I have to alter my consumption philosophy and lifestyle? To clear my head, I decided to apply for a week-long leave from work. I emailed my leave application and stayed back on my couch, sulking.

They were many things that I did not know and my information network was incapacitated by my father. This thought made my condition more distressing.

Looking at my sulky and curiosity-laden face, my father handed over a piece of paper to me. It was a note written in Junior Mrs. Bountiful's handwriting and addressed to my father: It was difficult to part with belongings of my lost child. Your blessings made it easier. I checked my tears. One might not agree with her approach towards waste, but it was impossible to remain untouched by the steadfastness of her belief. Instead of shaking her sincerity, adversities had made her stronger and wiser.

Meanwhile, my father asked my wife to bring the parcel to the other room. After reading the note and overcoming my emotions, I peeped inside that room. The parcel was opened and my wife was crying. They were new-born baby clothes, toys and utility products. All these items were packed with care so that they could be preserved forever. Looking at them, one could easily deduce how difficult it had been for Junior Mrs. Bountiful to give them away. I wiped my tears and withdrew from the room.

The next morning there was another parcel. This time, my father was the sender and Junior Mrs. Bountiful was the receiver. I could neither inform my father about my week-long leave nor could I disobey him. So, I took the parcel and left for the Bountiful house.

No one in the Bountiful family mentioned my leave application, nor did they question me when I left for my home early. However, a surprise awaited me the following morning.

When I reached the drawing room in my pyjamas, I found Junior Mrs. Bountiful and her daughter sitting with my son, daughter and wife. No one was speaking. My father motioned for me to bring water and I realised that nothing had been served to the visitors.

While laying the tray on the table I observed that their eyes were swollen. Junior Mrs. Bountiful was holding my wife's hand and both were comforting each other. My father blessed the lady, not as a subordinate, but as an elder.

My email was unusual and the lady had gauged my anxiety. She visited my home to put my doubts to rest. Junior Mrs. Bountiful knew how to win not just loyalty, but the devotion from employees. I was standing cautiously, considering whether it was the right time to accept subjugation or resist the inevitable change in my lifestyle for a little while longer.

* * *

At night, when we were in our bed, I spoke to my wife.

"All of you woke up early in the morning. It's unusual," I told her.

"Dad woke us up," she replied.

"Why didn't he wake me up?"

This time, instead of answering, she asked a question.

"Did you see what Junior Mrs. Bountiful and Baby Bountiful were wearing?"

It was a strange question after the tear-jerking morning.

"I can only recall that both of them were as elegant and well-dressed as they had always been. I'm sure Junior Mrs. Bountiful hasn't changed her designer team after coming back from her exile," I replied.

"The day before yesterday, dad showed me the parcel he received from Junior Mrs. Bountiful. She sent all the treasured items that were bought for her lost child. She wanted me to give away those items to other infants who can use them," said my wife.

Before I could express my thoughts, she continued.

"Yesterday morning, dad sent our children's and my old clothes to the lady. Both mother and daughter Bountiful were wearing those clothes after a few alterations," she said.

'What!'

I was shocked into silence. Firstly, I realised that Junior Mrs. Bountiful did not visit us to nurse my anxiety but to show off her and her daughter's dresses. Secondly, I did not intend to water down my wife's elation by telling her that, for making these few alterations in the dresses, Bountiful aides and designers must have toiled the whole day and had a sleepless night. I had seen them spending hours and days finalising fabric, embellishments and embroidery. Still, there was no denying that the rich lady had an enormously big heart. Otherwise, it would have been difficult to wear a dress made from clothes worn and discarded by an employee.

Some people feel an adrenaline rush from hunting animals. But have you ever seen an animal tamer? It is different from a circus where animals are aware that they are subjugated by the ringmaster. The real power lies in making people obey you and letting them believe that they are doing it out of their free will. Junior Mrs. Bountiful seemed to have acquired that kind of power and I had lost my last supporter, that is, my wife.

* * *

I was growing a lot more impatient to know what had transpired in the past couple of years. Thankfully, I got the go-ahead from my father to unplug the eyes and ears of my informers. I set the ball rolling as soon as my network was reactivated and revitalized. Muck Mound Slum was the precursor of the robust waste enterprise and I began my exploration from there.

I reached the office-cum-workshop that served as Junior Mrs. Bountiful's residence for one week. My companion, Mr. Candid, asked me to remove my shoes outside the room in which the lady spent the fateful week. It still had a bed with a soft mattress and the linen spread over it was sparkling clean. There was not a single crease either and the arrangement around the bed indicated religious attachment to the place.

Mr. Candid turned towards the bed and bowed with his folded hands. I also folded my hand and bowed, but the absence of a picture or an idol confused me.

To relieve my confusion, Mr. Candid took me for a round and

asked me to peek inside some of the slum dwellings. There was a wide contrast between the exteriors and interiors of the dwellings. The exteriors of Muck Mound slum were pauperized to evoke sympathy, but gains from Junior Mrs. Bountiful's initiatives were preserved inside homes, away from the prying eyes of the world.

Each of these houses had placed a miniature replica of the bed with a mattress and clean linen.

"Their clothes may remain unwashed for days, but the linen of their palm-sized beds are washed every day as a mark of respect for the lady benefactor," Mr. Candid told me.

We moved to another house that turned out to be Mr. Candid's home. Even there, I found incense sticks in front of a miniature bed.

"Everyone prays and seeks her blessings," said Mr. Candid.

I was baffled by the idea of a bed becoming a deity.

"People from other slums also visit our Bed Temple," he continued.

The Deity liked items made from discarded material the most. Devotees made offerings depending upon their reverence for the Goddess and what they sought from her. The Goddess who was worshipped through a symbolic, luxurious clean bed had a well-established system to fulfil the wishes of her devotees. Anyone who prayed for an upgrade in life was contacted by one of the Waste Priests. These devotees were enrolled in the Waste Co-operative according to their capabilities and received profits proportionately.

For the sake of clarity, let me first apprise you about what happened at the slum during Junior Mrs. Bountiful's hiding.

* * *

Mr. Candid believed that Junior Mrs. Bountiful should not stay at Muck Mound Slum. But he was filled with remorse because of humiliating accusations levelled against her. He began to light incense sticks in front of the lady's bed left at the office-cum-workshop and offered items made from waste to do his penance. The family of the dog-bitten baby and a few others similarly followed Mr. Candid to serve their penance.

Mr. Candid and Mr. Canny had developed a tacit understanding by then. While pauperizing the slum to escape the eviction, both of them converted the office-cum-workshop into the Waste Deity Temple and encouraged the slum people to pray there. Offerings and prayers were carried out around the bed. It was no longer an ordinary bed, but the totem that carried the spirit of their Waste Deity.

On the first anniversary of Junior Mrs. Bountiful's expulsion from Muck Mound Slum, a fair was organised at the Bed Temple. After seeking blessings from the Waste Deity, the devotees exchanged gifts made of waste materials. It was the beginning of a belief that the spirit of the Waste Goddess was passed from the giver of the gift to the recipient. They became waste-kin and their bond was unbreakable.

Junior Mrs. Bountiful brought a little prosperity and ample hope of improvement in the life of Muck Mound residents. These residents, however, expelled her from their slum due to the fear of losing their homes. After the eviction notice was cancelled, they were overwhelmed with insecurity and guilt. Blessings of the Waste Deity and the formation of waste kinship brought much-needed solace for them. The new waste business model reaped the benefits of their togetherness.

Different types of waste handlers and professionals within Dupli City were becoming a part of the waste business model. To eliminate competing against each other, Junior Mrs. Bountiful established a single registration and marketing body for all these entities. This was how the Waste Co-operative formed under the able guidance of the astute lady. The co-operative optimized efforts and resources required for market expansion.

A fair was again organised at the Bed Temple on the second anniversary and Waste Deity merchandise was introduced. It was collectively decided to declare this day as Penance Day and the fair became an annual event.

Someone who suffered and rose above her sufferings was revered and worshipped. One may debate whether Junior Mrs. Bountiful deserved to be a Goddess or not, but one could not deny her ability to convert challenges into opportunities.

I had heard that twenty-first-century wars will be fought with religious appropriation and soul harvesting. Here, I witnessed how these two things were effectively being utilised to build a system in which people were motivated to generate wealth by waging war against waste.

Chapter 10

THE WASTE-FULL JOURNEY

Junior Mrs. Bountiful was now firmly settled in the Bountiful home and had not left it for a couple of years. Dr. Nestor and Dr. Spunk, the fungal researchers, were still working to find a cure for Callousa Attapata, the fungus that killed Bountiful infant. They were satisfied with the renewed impoverishment of Muck Mound Slum. They were also impressed with Junior Mrs. Bountiful's unrelenting zeal to create better work opportunities for waste workers without meddling with their surroundings.

Junior Mrs. Bountiful's steadfast adherence to the cause, overlooking the humiliating expulsion from Muck Mound Slum, impelled Dr. Nestor and Dr. Spunk to visit the Bed Temple. The two fungal experts joined their hands and closed their eyes to pray at the place where Junior Mrs. Bountiful had once stayed to fight for bettering the poor condition of slum dwellers.

The story of compassion and perseverance of the Waste Goddess was no longer confined within the boundaries of Dupli City. It travelled with Dr. Nestor and Dr. Spunk to various slums in different parts of the world. The story was retold so many times that a few magical elements were inadvertently incorporated into it. There were reports of apparition of the deity. Some devotees also claimed that their wishes were fulfilled and diseases were cured. These reports and claims established divinity of the Waste Goddess beyond questioning.

The Waste Deity was not prospering alone. The Waste Co-operative also expanded its reach. The success stories of its members attracted more people towards the co-operative. Their success, however, was not without its problems.

Municipal concessionaires of waste-to-energy plants were not getting enough waste to run their plants. They threatened the Municipal Authority of Dupli City (MAD) to fulfil their contractual obligation of facilitating the smooth functioning of the plants or face litigation.

Until now, the progress of the Waste Co-operative had not bothered the MAD. Its efficient work ensured that Dupli City achieved a better ranking on the solid waste management index. Its services also enjoyed full support from residents and other establishments of the city. These people did not let the MAD replace the co-operative with concessionaires' waste collectors. In such a scenario, municipal officials could think of only one way to solve their problem—do away with the Waste Co-operative by hitting it at its roots.

Once again, a notice was served to demolish Muck Mound Slum. This time, the target was not a rich young lady, but the temple of the revered Deity. The Municipal Authority of Dupli City (MAD) overlooked this difference and forgot that living beings can be challenged, but not their faith. The slum residents, who shunned Junior Mrs. Bountiful to save their dwellings, lined up in front of the Waste Deity Temple, ready to lay their lives. Devotees of the Goddess were silent and motionless. Bulldozers, the police force and municipal officials stood idle and failed to trample down the Bed temple.

In the evening, the next set of devotees replaced the first set. The replacement process was repeated the following morning. There was one noticeable change, though. The Deity, in her human form, was sitting amidst her devotees.

Junior Mrs. Bountiful might not consider herself a Goddess, but her presence amplified the devotional fervour of silent protesters. They began to move towards the lady Goddess to seek blessings. However, the lady knew that further amplification of devotion might be detrimental to their cause. She made a gesture, indicating her desire to leave the slum. Her two lieutenants, Mr. Candid and Mr. Canny, cleared the path and the lady left.

The brief appearance of the Goddess reinforced her devotees' resolve to protect the temple and the slum. They resumed their quiet and motionless protest. Municipal officials and cops realised that removing such kind of protesters would earn them only brickbats. They left the place by the end of the second day.

Two days later, water and electricity supplies of waste workshops and other premises were disrupted. Warehouses were raided and sealed and licences were cancelled. Mr. Candid and Mr. Canny were jailed and put on trial for misappropriation of waste. Once again, a smear campaign was launched against Junior Mrs. Bountiful; this time by projecting the Waste Co-operative as a waste mafia.

When Junior Mrs. Bountiful came out of jail after meeting her trusted lieutenants, she found many press reporters waiting for her. There was another set of a crowd that was burning a waste effigy and a miniature bed. They were shouting slogans against the Waste Co-operative and Bountifuls. Junior Mrs. Bountiful gazed at the crowd and addressed the press reporters.

"Let's sit somewhere and talk. I'll arrange transportation for those who need it," she said.

Her civility in a hostile circumstance surprised the reporters and, advertently or inadvertently, all of them accepted her invitation.

Junior Mrs. Bountiful was not averse to going inside the ghettos of poverty and she had garnered the faith of the people living there. Therefore, she had unrestricted access to these places. She brought the journalists to the dumpyard adjacent to Muck Mound Slum.

"By the end of this press conference, all of us will smell like a waste-picker," said one of the journalists in her colleague's ear, cringing at the prospect.

"If we begin to smell alike, we will stop despising them," remarked Junior Mrs. Bountiful. "If we begin to smell alike, we'll not try to uproot them."

The journalist straightened her nose and looked around. No one was looking at her except Junior Mrs. Bountiful. She was horrified at the possibility of sitting in front of a mind reader.

"Relax, in a few minutes your nose will get used to this smell," said Mrs. Bountiful.

This time, she kept her focus away from the perplexed journalist, who ended up being silent throughout the entire press conference.

"The Waste Co-operative is charged with misappropriation of waste and you went to meet the two leading accused in jail," a journalist spoke out. "Doesn't it indicate that you condone their illegal activities?"

"Hello, Mr. Stooge," greeted Junior Mrs. Bountiful.

The journalist had never interacted with the lady before and he was not even famous. So, he found it strange that Junior Mrs. Bountiful knew his name.

"I am waiting for your response to my greetings," said the lady.

"Good evening, Mrs. Bountiful," said Mr. Stooge.

"Coming back to your question, let me clarify my position. They're my team members and I won't hesitate to provide them with the best possible legal aid. Let judiciary decide whether they've committed any crime or not."

"Establishing the Waste Deity was an act of generating passion. Do you understand that passion may kill you or make you a killer?"

"Passion also instils dedication and perseverance that are required to overcome difficulties in pursuit of your goals," responded Junior Mrs. Bountiful.

"It seems you're stirring up the passion to establish a monopoly in solid waste management of Dupli City," said Mr. Stooge.

"Monopolies are established to reap profits. Do you believe that solid waste management is a profitable business?" asked Junior Mrs. Bountiful.

Mr. Stooge did not answer her question but the lady did not let the matter slide.

"The Municipal Authority of Dupli City (MAD) charges a fee from waste generators and still fails to adopt efficient solid waste management practices. Unlike the MAD, the Waste Co-operative treats waste generators as its esteemed customers. We make solid waste management an easier and a more beneficial endeavour for everyone who is associated with it," she said. "No, we aren't aiming to establish a monopoly. On the contrary, the Waste Co-operative believe in collaboration and support. It's a mission to empower even the weakest member of the solid waste management hierarchy and it will not be restricted to Dupli City."

"Aren't you undermining the contribution of the MAD in managing the waste of Dupli City for all these years?" asked Mr. Stooge.

His voice was slightly lower because he was losing his ground to Mrs. Bountiful.

"Let me tell you why waste is piling up in dumpyards despite the MAD's contribution. The MAD is commissioning waste processing plants without adequate know-how. The objective of their awareness campaigns is to fulfil the official obligation, not to sensitize citizens.

Tens of penalty slips are issued to waste offenders and thousands of offenders are left scot-free because the entire citizenry can't be penalized. Moreover, these initiatives are abandoned as soon as there's a change in administrative priority. In a few years, and sometimes even in a few months, the money and effort invested in initial pomp and show are lost. While, in less than five years, our Waste Co-operative is standing on its own and is working successfully."

"Aren't you and the Waste Co-operative responsible for shutting down municipal waste-to-energy plants due to the lack of waste supply?" asked Mr. Stooge.

This time, meekness absolutely replaced his aggressive posturing.

"We're merely facilitating conversion of trash into treasure," answered the lady. "Shutting down anything or troubling anyone isn't our intention."

The lady looked at Mr. Stooge and smiled.

"Nobody has paid me anything to ask these questions," the journalist mumbled. He must have felt guilty for accepting undue favour from municipal waste concessionaire.

After receiving a nudge from the person sitting beside him, Mr. Stooge came back to his senses. Junior Mrs. Bountiful was still smiling and waiting for him to speak.

Junior Mrs. Bountiful had money and the people's support. Her position conferred privileges and constraints. She used both to her advantage. However, she did not spend her time and energy pulling people down. Mr. Stooge was intimidated when he failed in his attempt to intimidate. He took a deep breath and tried to say something. Nothing, however, came out of his mouth.

"Solid waste management is a costly affair and you are reaping profits. Is the whole world stupid or are you doing it wrong?" asked another journalist, Mr. Carper.

"While everyone is treating waste as a problem, the Waste Co-operative is treating it as treasure and that makes all the difference," answered Junior Mrs. Bountiful.

"Aren't you using poor waste-pickers for your gain by projecting yourself as their messiah?"

"It would have bothered me, had you accused me of misusing them," Junior Mrs. Bountiful said, with a hint of a smile. "I accept that I use them. And instead of pitying them, I make them work because I know their worth."

"Do you also accept promoting consumerism?"

"I do. Consumerism is the backbone of our successful model. People like to spend money and we've simply altered what they were paying for earlier. I believe that our approach helps in better management of solid waste."

"The Waste Co-operative is attracting followers by selling its success stories. Have you ever bothered to know the negative impacts of your initiative?"

"The Waste Co-operative is thriving because we act upon feedback and we have left the work of publicising our failures or sorrow stories for our detractors."

"Great. And how much does your family contribute to your success?" asked Mr. Carper, with his voice heavily loaded with sarcasm.

"Their support has made it look like a cakewalk," answered Junior Mrs. Bountiful.

Her eyes penetrated the journalist and he lost his composure

"The whole family is using each other for mutual benefit," he commented.

"I don't mind using people, be it waste-pickers or my family members. And I'm happy if they use me because it implies that I, too, am useful. All of us know that useless things are thrown in dustbins and end up in landfills."

"You can act innocent because your husband and mother-in-law cover your misdeeds."

"I won't try to dissuade you from finding faults because cynicism can't be separated from those who practise it," said Junior Mrs. Bountiful, terminating her interaction with the obnoxious journalist.

The microphone was now handed over to another journalist.

"You embarked on a solid waste management journey after losing your child. Does your loss still make you sorrowful?" asked Ms. Savvy.

Her question reminded Junior Mrs. Bountiful of the past few years. A cheerful smile spread on her face, devoid of sorrow. However, she appealed to the journalist not to ask personal questions.

After touching the right chord in the heart of the influential lady, Ms. Savvy smartly moved on to tricky issues.

"What are manufacturers doing to fulfil their obligation under Extended Producers Responsibility except for submitting recycling certificates?" asked the journalist.

"What else are they expected to do?" countered Junior Mrs. Bountiful with a question.

"As per the legislation on Extended Producers Responsibility, the manufacturer is responsible for the entire life-cycle of a product—its after-use collection, recycling and disposal. Its main purpose is to persuade manufacturers to adopt an innovative design for their products and packaging so that the quantity of material recovery is increased and the ill effects of waste on our environment are decreased.

However, manufacturers are obtaining mandatory certificates from those firms which are subletting the work to the unorganised sector, leading to unscientific and harmful practices of resource recovery. Through these firms, manufacturers have found an easy route to meet the legislative requirement, circumventing the aim of design innovation."

"It's good that you've done your homework well. Would you like to put in a little more effort?"

"It's difficult to trust your intentions because you are hand-in-glove with people who are illegally importing waste. Is the health and well-being of our waste handlers inconsequential?" asked the journalist.

"I choose not to pick up futile confrontations and wait for an appropriate time for each action," Junior Mrs. Bountiful said, taking a deep breath. "I am with you to put an end to this practice as long as you are not selective in naming and shaming people who work in the industry."

Apparently, Ms. Savvy understood that running a successful business without being selective in moral alignments is next to impossible. But she could not reconcile with the tacit understanding between the Waste Co-operative and Foeman Plastic Factory which heavily depended on exported waste. After all, exported waste sometimes contained human body parts. Rich countries were not being inhumane to carry out such acts deliberately, but errors occurred. The stink from these body parts was unbearable by the time it reached the destination country and might have infected its waste workers. The destination country often traded off between health and economic advantage while accepting or rejecting the consignment.

"Overthinking is detrimental to decision-making," Junior Mrs.

Bountiful said, understanding Ms. Savvy's dilemma. "You've already gathered a lot of information in this field and have great potential to learn even more. I invite you to join my team."

"So that no one questions you for promoting Green Capitalism in the garb of Green Socialism?" the journalist asked, unwilling to relent.

"So that you can witness how things are managed at the Waste Co-operative and report the facts," said Junior Mrs. Bountiful. "I extend my invitation once again and request you not to refuse it. You might regret foregoing this opportunity later on in your life."

Someone else might have treated Junior Mrs. Bountiful's invitation as a threat but the wise journalist grabbed the opportunity. She smiled. Junior Mrs. Bountiful smiled with her. Making allies was one of Mrs. Bountiful's ways to exterminate her opposition.

Miss Axe Effect, the lady detective, appeared at the back of the press conference and Mr. Peeptown sat with one of the journalists. Mr. Peeptown was still meeting people and connecting them for their mutual benefit. As far as I know, he was the one who brought Mr. Candid and Mr. Canny together to save the residents of Muck Mound Slum from eviction and to establish the Waste Co-operative. He was doing it through the instructions issued by Junior Mrs. Bountiful.

Mr. Peeptown was instrumental in many other waste collaborations, a few of which I will narrate at suitable moments. Miss Axe Effect was not visible in public as much as Mr. Peeptown. However, her inputs were evident in Junior Mrs. Bountiful's strategy and actions.

I could not say whether Junior Mrs. Bountiful's ability to read minds was self-acquired or borrowed from Miss Axe Effect. But I knew that Miss Effect was extracting and dispensing information to help Mrs. Bountiful in foreseeing and removing a hurdle before it got out of hand. Information mining was also a crucial tool for creating a story. The Waste Story was spreading far and wide because its propagator knew how to employ truth effectively.

* * *

Devotees of the Waste Deity intensified their protest after watching videos of effigy burning outside the jail. Waste generators, workers, processors and consumers—everyone associated with waste was protesting. After all, those effigies of waste and the miniature bed were symbols of their beloved Goddess.

The press conference also worked as an effective catalyst. People, not only from Dupli City but every part of the globe, were lending their support irrespective of their understanding of the subject matter. The downtrodden background of the two prisoners stimulated their emotions.

Within a few days, the Municipal Authority of Dupli City (MAD) began to feel the pressure from the protests. A meeting between Junior Mrs. Bountiful and the Municipal Officer, Mr. Swindler ensured the release of Mr. Candid and Mr. Canny from jail. Amidst the chants condemning waste imperialism in favour of waste democracy, both the prisoners came out with folded hands, humbled by the support they were receiving.

* * *

Meanwhile, Mr. Stooge alighted from the car that dropped him at his home after the press conference. The journalist entered his house and, before closing the door, he looked around. There was no one in his house. He switched on a light and settled on a sofa. After a few phone calls and writing notes, he went towards his window to get some fresh air. They were a few unexpected shadows.

After a few days of vigil, Mr. Stooge felt that he was being watched and his actions were controlled by people at his work and personal space. He had been diagnosed with paranoia. When changing psychiatrists could not change the diagnosis, Mr. Stooge stopped spending his money on them. However, he kept his belief of being watched and controlled.

Chapter 11

The Journey Continues

During the press conference, Ms. Savvy had mentioned the alleged liaison between the Waste Co-operative and Foeman Plastic Factory. Many of the readers might have forgotten Mr. Foeman. So, let me provide a quick peek at Mr. Foeman's business and his connection with the Waste Co-operative.

Mr. Foeman is the business rival of the Bountiful family. The Bountiful and Foeman families had FMCG companies that make them competitors. Besides that, Mr. Foeman had cement plants, an infrastructure development company and plastic manufacturing factories. The media kept on comparing the financial and social stature of both business houses, thereby, giving the impression of intense rivalry between them. They might have played games of one-upmanship, but no serious case of sabotage had ever come to light from either side.

Foeman Plastic Factory recycled plastic waste. In the absence of an adequate domestic supply, Mr. Foeman had been utilising imported plastic waste for a couple of decades. Their incentives and profit margins fared better in doing so.

Times were changing, but changing a decades-old system needed a huge motivation or counter-incentive. Environmental activists had succeeded in pursuing the government to ban waste import, but they did not have the means to check misrepresentation, falsification or fraud. Consequently, legal import was now replaced by the illegal import of waste.

* * *

After the success of Waste Phone App and waste-to-product initiatives, Junior Mrs. Bountiful called Mr. Peeptown to arrange a meeting with Mr. Foeman. She was no longer just a business person, but the Waste Deity who commanded the devotion of waste workers. Mr. Foeman readily agreed to pay a visit to her.

"I am a fierce competitor but, more than that, I am an astute businessman," he announced.

"Then, we must join forces in ensuring each other's growth. In the areas of conflict, we can choose separate paths without creating obstacles for each other," said Junior Mrs. Bountiful removing the scope for animosity between them.

In the initial days of their collaboration, Mr. Foeman's indulgence with imported plastic waste was under waste warriors' radar but they chose the path of no confrontation.

"Junior Mrs. Bountiful doesn't encourage illegal waste import, but she understands that securing a livelihood for waste-pickers is more important," defended Mr. Peeptown during one of the Waste Co-operative meetings. "Moreover, plastic waste found on our streets is equally contaminated."

It was easier for Junior Mrs. Bountiful to keep calm and focus on her goal. Apart from her devotees, she was shielded by people surrounding her. She, in turn, protected everyone with all her might.

The Waste Co-operative began an employment exchange. It helped waste handlers in finding employment at ports where imported plastic waste was unloaded and at Foeman Plastic Factory which used this waste for manufacturing plastic goods.

Mr. Foeman framed guidelines for workers' protection. The army of waste warriors who could have been fighting against him because of illegal import of plastic waste were instead assisting him in processing the imported waste. Consequently, Foeman Plastic

Factory and the associated recyclers had been reaping benefits.

Junior Mrs. Bountiful implored Bountiful Company Board to take up the responsibility of channelling domestic plastic waste under Corporate Social Responsibility and Extended Producers Responsibility. But unlike imported waste, domestic plastic waste was scattered in many places. Instead of getting it collected from the streets, Bountiful Company Board empanelled a few non-profit organizations to collect domestic plastic waste from homes, markets and institutes. Foeman Company Board replicated the model and it set in the domino effect. Subsequently, many other companies, big and small, adopted Bountiful and Foeman's model.

Beggars and street vendors were roped in to keep a check on people who threw waste on move. Very few people paid heed because these waste warriors lacked ammunition. Streets continued to receive trash until a few warriors converted themselves into outlaws. They began snatching packages and plastic bottles before these items could be thrown. There was a supporting network to trace the whereabouts of waste offenders. Pictures of these offenders were clicked while throwing waste and were pasted at their residences, workplaces and vehicles. One might call them waste vigilantes—a terror for those who scatter waste but saviours of cleanliness and wellbeing.

Foeman Plastic Factory was also one of the major beneficiaries of domestic plastic waste collection. The Bountiful and Foeman friendship stood on solid piles of waste and these piles rose so high that Mr. Foeman did not have to import waste anymore. However, it did not mean that exporting and importing waste had ceased in Dupli City.

* * *

The release of Mr. Canny and Mr. Candid from jail was another turning point in the waste-full journey. Old rules were forsaken to make space for a new set of rules.

Before working for Junior Mrs. Bountiful, Mr. Canny and his gang used to smuggle waste from slaughterhouses, hospitals and industries to dump it on municipal landfills in connivance with municipal staff. On the other hand, Mr. Candid had interacted extensively with Dupli City's waste workers whether they belonged to government machinery or were private players. While working as a waste contractor, he had always been a silent yet keen observer. Therefore, Mr. Canny could secure a foothold in the dark underbelly of waste mafia and Mr. Candid gained good traction among over-ground waste workers.

Mr. Mender, who was the solid waste management in-charge of Bountiful premises, was now involved in resolving waste processing issues. Mr. Peeptown and Miss Axe Effect had also been associated with Junior Mrs. Bountiful before the conception of the Waste Co-operative. The gentleman was good at facilitating communications, coordinating activities of the Co-operative and building mutually beneficial relationships. The lady detective discovered facts and extracted information that helped in many wonderful ways besides winning over people.

Junior Mrs. Bountiful valued people who could act. Having good intentions with no courage, capability or willpower to work served no purpose. Her team was continuously replenished with members who could pull off any intended task.

All sorts of efforts were activated to tame the opposition. No one was classified as a friend or foe but as a facilitator or detractor. The task at hand was to convert detractors into facilitators. While parameters of idealism were changing, the scope and clout of the Waste Co-operative were ascending at a much faster pace.

* * *

In the past few days, the Sustainability Tribunal had penalised many municipal authorities throughout the country for failing to ensure an effective solid waste management system. The tribunal directed state governments to pay heavy environmental compensation for damaging the environment and public health due to the mismanagement of waste.

Dupli City also appeared in the list of offenders. Besides inefficient solid waste management, the Municipal Authority of Dupli City (MAD) was also accused of fudging data and facts. For example, documents submitted to the Sustainability Tribunal stated that 90% of the solid waste generated in Dupli City was processed, while according to the cleanliness survey, only 55% of solid waste was processed. The MAD clarified that the documents submitted to the tribunal indicated waste processing data from the previous year. It further argued that the cleanliness survey was conducted after solid waste management of Dupli City was adversely affected by untoward circumstances prevailing in the past few months. The MAD representative did not elaborate on what the untoward circumstances were nor did the judges of the tribunal questioned him in this regard. Everyone was aware of the conflict between the MAD on behalf of its waste concessionaires and the Waste Co-operative.

Further, the Sustainability Tribunal stayed the proposal for the expansion of waste-to-energy plants because these plants had failed to adhere to green norms. The tribunal also reprimanded the MAD for non-compliance of their previous order in which it directed the municipal authority to ensure the provision of bio-methanation or ingesta plants at slaughterhouses to treat cattle paunch and animal waste along with the provision of effluent treatment plants for 100% recirculation of their wastewater. However, in the past year, fewer than required bio-methanation plants and no effluent treatment plant, were constructed. To hide their collective failure, slaughterhouses and the MAD were burying their waste at landfills in the dark hours of the night.

The drubbing of the Municipal Authority of Dupli City (MAD) by the Sustainability Tribunal was one of the major news headlines for a couple of days. Later, a few media outlets refused to let the news fizzle out. Day after day, they brought out new allegations against the municipal authority of the densely populated metropolis. These media outlets were alleged proxies of the Waste Co-operative.

Meanwhile, an NGO filed a litigation against the government order which allowed partial lifting of the ban on plastic waste import. The order permitted recyclers to import PET flakes, chunks and bottles. The NGO also raised alarm about a few shipments of suspected banned hazardous plastic waste. To placate them, the environment ministry directed ten private firms to furnish details of their plastic import. It was suspected that name of Foeman Plastic Factory had been included in the list of these firms at the behest of the Waste Co-operative's detractors. However, this news failed to gain traction and fizzled out in a day.

In response to the litigation filed by the NGO, the Sustainability Tribunal sounded caution for the environment ministry to test the credentials of the NGO. There was a high probability that they were working in cahoots with municipal waste concessionaires. The tribunal allowed the partial import of plastic waste and ruled that environmental protection had to be balanced with the livelihood of people employed in the recycling sector.

The Waste Co-operative had the upper hand and Mr. Swindler, the Municipal Officer, saw wisdom in disowning municipal waste concessionaires. After suspending a few municipal officials from their duty and blacklisting guilty waste concessionaires, he summoned Mr. Peeptown to fix a meeting with Junior Mrs. Bountiful. The benevolent lady arrived at the municipal office with Mr. Peeptown.

* * *

The Municipal Authority of Dupli City (MAD) leased out landfill sites to the Waste Co-operative. They also collaborated on the collection, sorting and resource recovery of waste. The co-operative used its already-established network of waste handlers, bio-methanation plants, incinerators and composting units to carry out these operations. In less than a month, the MAD began to earn by tying up with industries to clear refuse-derived fuel and inert waste from municipal waste processing sites. The Waste Co-operative also assisted the MAD in freeing up many thousands of square feet of space and earning over ten million rupees from the disposal of scrap scattered around municipal office premises.

City drains were no longer choking with waste and the streets became clean. The citizens' support also contributed to the improvement of the sanitary condition of Dupli City and the city ranked first in the cleanliness ranking. Better solid waste management had been achieved with the lesser deployment of municipal manpower and infrastructure. So, municipal employees were also celebrating their lighter workload.

Armed with drastic improvement on the ground and on paper, Junior Mrs. Bountiful's legal team helped the MAD win a penalty waiver from the Sustainability Tribunal. The name of Dupli City was also removed from the list of environmental offenders. Mr. Swindler, the municipal officer, expressed his gratitude to Mrs. Bountiful for her support.

Keeping in mind public sentiments and the persuasive feedback received from Mr. Swindler, elected members of the Municipal

Authority of Dupli City (MAD) called for a conference. The topics for discussion were to outline a futuristic solid waste management system and define role of waste-to-energy plants. Subject experts and chairman of the Sustainability Tribunal were also called for their valuable input.

* * *

Once the refreshments were served, the discussion began in full swing. One of the municipal committee members from opposition party accused MAD of leasing out the landfill sites to the Waste Cooperative at throwaway price.

"Earlier, the MAD was paying others to design, operate and maintain those landfills. Now it has generated revenue by leasing them out. They were leased out at a highly subsidised rate not to favour anyone, but to support environmental protection and earn carbon credits," answered Mr. Swindler.

When the subject of waste-to-energy plants came up, one of the experts put forward a few points to prove that technology X has the edge. The another one quickly countered this argument and presented technology Z as superior. Mr. Swindler smartly used the points and counter-points presented by the two experts to pull down both technologies. He questioned the need for any of the expensive and imprecise techniques.

Mr. Swindler's assault on technology irked Dr. Fervid, one of the experts.

"Researchers and experts burn their night oil to invent and improvise technology, not to satiate their vanity but for the betterment of the society," she said.

Mr. Swindler sympathised with her because he, too, was a great admirer of fanciful technologies. Before he could utter something detrimental to Junior Mrs. Bountiful's plan, the latter intervened.

"All of us marvel at state-of-the-art technologies, but simpler techniques must also be credited for solving problems," said Junior Mrs. Bountiful. "When we are short of funds and have an abundance of labour, shouldn't we choose cheaper and simpler solutions that can effectively employ our labour force?"

"True…true," said Mr. Swindler, resuming his support for Junior Mrs. Bountiful.

This made Dr. Fervid furious.

"Technological advancements have generated employment since the Industrial Revolution. Yet, you still consider it detrimental for poor people," she hit back at the rich lady. "Is it because you want them to remain poor?"

"The Industrial Revolution showcased unlimited human potential. Our technologies give us an edge over other species on the Earth and we can utilise Earth's resources at a faster pace than its generation capacity," said Junior Mrs. Bountiful. "Now is the time for another revolution. Now is the time to remake our products so that they continue to remain in circulation instead of getting dumped or burnt. For that, we need the support of our researchers and experts.

"Please lead the way in evolving manufacturing techniques."

All the attendees thumped their desks cheering the lady's passionate appeal. Dr. Fervid was overwhelmed by the importance given to the researchers and experts fraternity. She was ready to shoulder the responsibility of guiding humankind towards circular production techniques.

Dr. Frosty, the other expert, was visibly unmoved by the happenings in the meeting hall. When thumping stopped, he voiced his objections.

"I don't intend to cast aspersions on anyone. However, I would like to bring to everyone's notice that Mr. Swindler selectively picked a portion of my research paper to validate an unsuitable waste-to-energy technology and discard newer, more suitable technology. He overlooked other sections of my research paper that highlight the drawbacks of their chosen technology. I want to know whether his selection and omission were deliberate and carried out to favour a particular concessionaire," he said.

"Can you explain this?" Mr. Sardonic, chairman of the Sustainability Tribunal, asked Mr. Swindler. Mr. Swindler nodded and dug into the pile of documents he had brought with him.

"You have brought these huge bundles of paper to mislead us. I am sorry to disappoint you Mr. Swindler, but I am aware of your tricks," said Mr. Sardonic.

"It isn't my intention Sir," said Mr. Swindler, defending the allegation against him. "I did not know which paper you would ask for, so I brought all of them."

Almost all municipal officials had a reputation for misleading the tribunal and were considered incompetent and greedy. However, owing to Mr. Swindler's support for her mission, Junior Mrs. Bountiful turned towards Mr. Sardonic.

"We must respect each other's work," she said.

"When they managed their waste well, the tribunal waived their penalty. However, cleverness is an asset which they use to fool people," countered Mr. Sardonic. "They only work for personal gain."

"Everyone works for some gain," said Junior Mrs. Bountiful. "Some do it for money, some for fame or self-gratification and other kinds of favours."

"Respected lady, my job is to find fault with their work," said

Mr. Sardonic, standing up to leave. "If you and everyone else wish to give them a free hand, what's the use of inviting me for this meeting?"

"I understand your concern and appreciate it," Junior Mrs. Bountiful said, in an attempt to calm him down. "Please be seated and tell us how can we improve solid waste management in Dupli City."

"Implementation of solid waste management comes under the purview of municipal authorities. My job is to check them if and when they're going wrong," said Mr. Sardonic.

"Can't we find someone who can assist the MAD so that it doesn't go wrong too often?" asked the lady.

Mr. Sardonic looked at Dr. Fervid and Dr. Frosty, seeking their response.

"We can only provide solutions, but implementation comes under the MAD's domain. We can't even stop the MAD from going wrong because it's the tribunal's job," said Dr. Frosty, placing the onus back on Mr. Sardonic.

"How can we stop the MAD before it commits a mistake? We've to wait till it makes one," said Mr. Sardonic, defending the tribunal.

Meanwhile, Mr. Swindler had sorted out the documents and presented Dr. Frosty's research paper.

"The study analyses the pros and cons of various waste-to-energy technologies. The results of the analysis favour the new technology for better efficiency, but remains silent on the risk involved in implementing it.

"They're inadequate case studies and, therefore, on-ground effectiveness and safety of this new waste-to-energy technology can't be assessed accurately. Its implementation is also tricky due to lack of experienced minds and hands. If our contractor fails in its proper implementation, we'll be accused of being careless with public money and, in the worst scenario, we might even be accused of misappropriation for personal gains," Mr. Swindler explained.

"Even now, you are accused of colluding with your blacklisted waste concessionaires who were using old technology at municipal waste-to-energy plants," said Mr. Sardonic.

"Still, we're in a position to defend ourselves. Worldwide, that old technology is popular and its proven track record makes it a safe bet at the time of awarding contracts. As for the rest, we always welcome experts to change public perception by making them aware of upcoming technologies," Mr. Swindler responded.

Dr. Fervid got excited at the proposition. But, considering Dr. Frosty's tacit response, she too declined the invite and conceded that only the MAD had the authority to deal with the public.

"Ladies and gentlemen, cleverness is also an asset to manoeuvre around the public, their representatives, experts and their admirers," Mr. Swindler said, feeling triumphant after successfully defending himself and the entire the Municipal Authority of Dupli City (MAD).

The Municipal Committee members who were patiently hearing all sides thumped their desks in solidarity.

Chapter 12
United Nation of Wastedoms

With the approval from Municipal Committee, Junior Mrs. Bountiful and Mr. Swindler formalised a partnership between the Waste Co-operative and the Municipal Authority of Dupli City (MAD) to convert Dupli City into a Waste-Circuit City. Junior Mrs. Bountiful extended similar partnerships with municipal authorities of different towns and cities all over the world. These collaborations aimed at creating a circular economy through community building, resource and information sharing and policy intervention.

Municipal Chief Officers of all Waste-Circuit Cities welcomed the suggestion of introducing Waste Reutilisation Rating for manufactured products. But as usual, policy-making goes through its share of glitches and got delayed. To get the ball rolling, the Waste Co-operative took it upon itself to set up a Waste Reutilisation Standardization Bureau. The bureau codified a star-rating system for waste reutilisation that was based on the proportion of reused and recycled waste in manufacturing a product. Waste Circularity Tags issued by the bureau indicated star rating and related information of those products.

These tags proved beneficial for companies that were eager to attract environmentally conscious consumers. These consumers were willing to pay for certified sustainability, thereby, encouraging more and more companies to apply for Waste Circularity Tags. It paved the way for mandatory tagging through legislative enactment.

A few people were accusing lawmakers and enforcers, religious and social influencers, profit and not-for-profit organizations of subtly tilting the legislation and public opinion in favour of the Waste

Co-operative. It was rumoured that there was also a mercenary outfit. This outfit took pride in its disciplined cadre and discrete operations. It seldom used violence because its mere presence was enough to keep everything under control.

Creation and smooth functioning of Waste-Circuit Cities required favourable laws and policies and, their effective enforcement. Junior Mrs. Bountiful, the Waste Co-operative and their partners were simply working to achieve that goal. With their pragmatic approach, positive results began to show earlier than expected.

Research & Development fund allocation prioritised the flow of funds into research kitties of scientific institutions that were working on waste management, reduction and reutilisation. Production Linked Incentives were introduced for manufacturers and entrepreneurs to create circular manufacturing, where everything was a resource and nothing was discarded. The main motive was optimum utilisation of natural resources and reduction of waste disposal costs.

The unhindered flow of funds ensured that researchers focussed on decreasing waste generation, lowering waste toxicity, better management of unavoidable waste and waste-to-product/energy. Meanwhile, technocrats supported the cause by introducing artificial intelligence and robotic solutions along with conventional methods to improve solid waste management at manufacturing units. These machine-vision tools helped in identifying and sorting different types of waste, supply chain analytics, resource extraction from discarded products and green product designing.

Along with major players, individuals and smaller players ruled the roost with a little experimentation and innovation. A financially humble background did not prove to be a deterrent for many of these innovators. They were not only finding new ways to reuse plastic, paper, pens, metals, lights, glasses, and bottles, but a few of them also converted items like cigarette buds, Styrofoam, ceramics, and light bulbs into useful products.

People from rural areas in and around the city were not left behind either. In developed countries, major food wastage occurred between retail to consumers because of cosmetic and quality norms. In developing countries, food wastage happened between farm to retail due to poor packaging and transit management. An association of farm owners, supported by the Waste Co-operative and its industrial partners, was created to monitor proper storage, packaging and transportation of raw food. This association also worked towards the expansion of recycling and reuse activities of farm, food and dairy waste.

The hospitality industry showered discounts on guests who avoided disposable toiletries or cutlery. Organizations and individuals working towards minimizing cooked food waste were also encouraged to develop a collaborative-profitable model.

Waste was also coming back into our lives in the form of garden furniture, home interiors, recreational items and many non-load-bearing parts of a structure. Quality checks and pricing algorithms were helping in the resale of all kinds of pre-owned and refurbished items. Shops dedicated sections for refurbished, recycled and pre-loved goods. More and more shoppers were buying from these sections. People could not give up spending and they paid willingly once their pride was attached to their purchase.

Weavers wove fabric from waste, sculptors made carvings out of waste and a new breed of event managers enlivened our parties with discarded items. Stories on solid waste management were written and movies were made. All sorts of artists—musicians, dancers, sculptors, animators and others—used their art forms to convey the message of waste utilisation.

The Waste Co-operative and its city-specific subsidiaries sponsored concerts, exhibitions, tours, social and sports events to promote a waste culture that was inclusive of all sections of society. Religious leaders were roped in to preach sermon on importance of increasing waste circularity. Everyone believed that they were saviours of the land, water and air. Waste Crusader Awards were conferred to acknowledge exemplary service or performance of the highest order that included various fields of waste endeavour.

The digital repair movement was launched by various public-spirited individuals and organisations to address the e-waste problem. Consequently, right-to-repair rules were enacted. Manufacturers were now legally bound to make spare parts available, allow unlocking and modification of software of a device and adopt circular designs. Automated checks on refurbished device performance diminished the scepticism involved in their resale.

With the progress in waste processing, the cost of resource extraction and material reutilisation went down and it was hoped that soon it would be lesser than the cost of mining the earth for new material. Solid waste management and circularity came up as the new wealth-generation opportunity for industries, institutions and individuals.

Educational institutes designed new courses with a special focus on waste management and circularity. Few of them imparted short-term Special Training Course on Waste Diplomacy that was sponsored by the Waste Co-operative. This course involved modules on polity of various Waste-Circuit Cities; foreign policy of countries in which these cities were located; impact of solid waste management practices on their environment, health, economy; requirement of humanitarian assistance. It helped in developing a diplomatic protocol that had resulted in better co-ordination among Subsidiary

Waste Co-operatives of different Waste-Circuit Cities.

Subsequently, academicians developed a Waste Centric Curriculum. Schools aided by the Waste Co-operative and its city-specific subsidiaries followed this curriculum. They're history lessons on ancient methods and traditions that supported reduction, reuse and recycling of waste. In language classes, students learnt waste terminologies and concepts through alphabets, words, and sentence formations. Waste had become the pivot for teaching numerical jugglery or developing scientific temperament. Be it data on waste generation, reutilisation, and transportation or developing civic sense through various administrative bodies, students were growing up believing that our lives revolved around solid waste management and circularity.

* * *

Everyone was doing what they had always been doing. Each skill found its utility in the waste economy, then how could criminals and extremists be left aside?

When minor, yet frequent, cases of waste thefts and robberies occurred, no one reported them to the police. They did not want to become a laughing stock by lodging a formal complaint. Few people who overcame their hesitation were sent away by city cops because they did not consider it a serious crime.

It brought cheers to the waste community because it contributed towards the soaring price of waste. However, when the menace grew, people were discouraged from treasuring recyclable, reusable and compostable waste. The dire need to prevent and detect waste crimes resulted in the appointment of Waste Defenders. These Waste Defenders worked under the Waste Co-operative and Police Departments of Waste-Circuit Cities allowed them to deal with petty waste thefts and robberies.

While minor waste crimes were declining, serious criminal offences found its foothold in the waste world. Even though criminal creativity is an indispensable part of society, it offended the normal sensitivities of society.

Waste propagandists held human beings responsible for burgeoning waste. Extremists among them believed that the solution to this problem laid in extinction of the entire specie of homo sapiens from the face of the earth. In some parts of the world, lynching of suspected waste offenders was reported.

Waste gangs were also mushrooming throughout Waste-Circuit Cities. Each gang aspired to increase its area of influence and this resulted in gang wars. Advertently or inadvertently, the Waste Deity Temple was defiled in one of their skirmishes and riots broke out in Dupli City. Junior Mrs. Bountiful grieved for the deaths and destruction, condemning riots but not the rioters.

They were whispers that it could have been a rival's job who wished to usurp the invisible throne of the Waste Co-operative. Another rumour surfaced that there was a covert rivalry between the two trusted lieutenants. Different people believed different possibilities as true, but I was confident that neither Mr. Canny nor Mr. Candid would encourage defiling of their beloved deity. Mr. Foeman was also a sensible fellow who understood his limitations and opportunities.

During these riots, a pregnant lady's stomach was accidentally slit with a knife. Her child burst out of her womb and landed on the Waste Deity's feet. Nobody knew the whole truth about the incident, but everyone knew about the miraculous escape of the baby, the baby born with the blessings of the Waste Goddess.

The dead lady was declared the first waste-martyr and her

poverty ensured that her martyrdom was unquestionable. Her statue was erected at the spot where she suffered martyrdom.

* * *

Process of creating cults, building statues, and naming or renaming build public memory that continues to live on for many generations. Waste-Circuit Cities were renamed as Wastedoms. City X was now called Wastedom X and City Y was now called Wastedom Y and so on. In these cities, elections were lost or won on the basis of waste circulation and management status.

Collectively, all these Wastedoms came under the administrative control of the Waste Co-operative and were called the United Nation of Wastedoms (UNW). The UNW was a borderless nation, united by the ideology of waste circulation and Junior Mrs. Bountiful was its undisputed ruler.

There were multiple routes to get the coveted citizenship of United Nation of Wastedoms (UNW), a country within many countries. These routes were:

Invest or donate to authorised waste enterprises or organizations.

Donate land to UNW.

Purchase national bonds of UNW.

A new crop of citizenship brokers emerged who facilitated the process.

The failure of general police force to rein in notorious waste crimes in Waste-Circuit Cities and the increase in pendency of waste cases led to the formation of Waste Police and the setting up of Waste Courts. These institutes had legal sanctity to settle waste crimes and disputes. Waste Defenders, who were appointed to deal with petty waste crimes, were merged with Waste Police.

A Waste Military was set up to deal with borderless waste

threats or aggression, exert the influence of UNW and propagate its objectives. Waste Diplomats were appointed in various countries to negotiate waste trade deals, tackle waste disputes, carry out humanitarian assistance during waste crisis and implement waste policies. Various other waste ministries and their executive wings were established for the smooth functioning and safeguarding the interest of UNW.

To consolidate the economic gains and augment them further, Waste Central Bank was established. Waste Currency was issued and regulated by the Bank and various kinds of financial institutions functioned under its ambit. From time to time Waste Central Bank released Waste Bonds to raise funds for waste projects. Companies or institutions could avail this fund based on their 'material circularity score'.

Waste Trade Federation was set up to create a worldwide waste-based economy. Its acronym, WTF offended some and amused others, but no one gave a f*** about proposing a change of its name.

* * *

Be it technocrats and entrepreneurs or artists and civic employees, everyone worshipped the Waste Deity for one reason or another. Poor and not-so-rich people were bowing before her as the source of motivation and well-being. The affluent populace popularised her as the Goddess of Empathy to reflect that rich people were also capable of compassion and kindness.

Waste gangs and waste criminals worshipped the Waste Deity as the source of ruthless power. They organised punching contests annually in which participants punch each other till one of the contestants got hurt. Blood is then smeared on the idol of the Goddess and everyone sought her blessing.

Dr. Nestor and Dr. Spunk, the two fungal experts, presented their drug development data to Bountiful Pharmaceutical Company and it ensured a cure from the Callousa Attapata. Junior Mrs. Bountiful made this data available in the public domain. It gained many devotees for the Waste Deity among researchers and the medical fraternity. This apart, anyone who feared catching a fungal infection or wanted a cure for it, brought an offering to the Bed Temple. Personally, it was a relief for me because after beginning my story with a fungus, I had been wishing it to resurface in this story.

The Waste Deity became the goddess of the rich and the poor, the law-abiding citizens and the outlaws, the elites and the masses, the meek and the powerful, the healthy and the unwell. One Bed Temple could not contain the rush of devotees. Therefore, more temples came up in various Wastedom Cities.

www.ingramcontent.com/pod-product-compliance
Lightning Source LLC
LaVergne TN
LVHW090219180726
843492LV00012B/2009